Pellitory Books

Living Memory

J.R. Martin

PELLITORY

Published 2011
Story Books
Springfield Terrace
East-the-Water
Bideford
Devon
EX39 4AN

ISBN 978-0-9553802-2-8

© J.R. Martin

Living Memory

J.R.Martin

All rights reserved. No part of this publication may be reproduced,
stored in a retrieval system, or transmitted in any form by any means
electronic, mechanical, photocopying, scanning, recording or otherwise,
without the prior written permission of the publishers.

Typeset, printed and bound by
Lazarus Press
Caddsdown Business Park
Bideford
Devon
EX39 3DX
www.lazaruspress.com

For C.H.

1

My attention was drawn to a middle-aged man and woman who were leaning on the bridge parapet, shielding their eyes from the afternoon sun as they look down at the incoming tidal flow.

"Look at all that filth!" remarked the man. He pointed to the undulating slick of creamy, light brown foam being carried along by the water as it skimmed the muddy sand.

The woman agreed and added: "I don't know how those kids can play about in that mucky water." She was referring to some youngsters in the distance, two in kayaks, the rest swimming. "It's sewage, isn't it?"

I stood a few feet to their left, looking in the same direction. I had paused to look at the same foam, the interesting fractal patterns, branching and re-joining, curling and swirling. I wondered: shall I bother to say anything? I'd explained to people about this before. Perhaps I shall - they're probably here on holiday and they might enjoy it more if I can change their negative perception of the water in the estuary.

I stepped closer. "Excuse me. I couldn't help over-hearing your conversation just then. That scum - it isn't sewage, you know, and it's not pollution - it's just an alga that lives on the surface of the mud." I paused; they might not recognise the word 'alga'. The poster in the information centre about this seasonal algal bloom uses the more familiar plural 'algae'. I mentioned the poster and added "You get it in the summer. It's quite natural."

The man's response was a look of hostile suspicion. "Is that what they say it is? It looks like sewage to me." I gave up and turned away to continue walking across the bridge.

A young woman with blonde hair had just crossed the road from the other side and was walking ahead of me. Suddenly I was startled by a whiff of memory. What was that scent? It was floral, old-fashioned, not at all rampant, or spicy - the way present-day perfumes seemed to me. I walked a little quicker in order to keep up with her, wondering if I could I ask her what it was. I began to lose confidence - she'd probably think I'm odd, a creepy old man.

But, as I drew nearer, I recognised her as someone I knew slightly. "Janice?" She stopped and turned round. "I haven't seen you for a long time. How are you? How are your mum and dad?" We talked for a minute or so. Then, when it was time to part I asked: "What's that nice scent?"

She was puzzled - she wasn't aware of any particular 'fragrance' she was wearing. Then she remembered: "Oh, it must be this." She held her wrist close to my nose. "I don't know what it's called - it's something my grandma found in a drawer."

Later that afternoon I was sitting in the shade in my garden overlooking the estuary, reading. I looked up - something had caught my attention. There was a change in the air. High water. I had found, soon after moving to that house, that you can often sense the turning of the tide.

I closed my book, stood up and walked across to look over the sea wall. On the way back I noticed that the wind, from its new direction, carried the scent of French marigolds from my neighbour's garden. A happy smell - a reminder, along with other flowers such as buddleia and privet, of summer holidays. I wondered: why am I so aware of smells today? I thought of that 'found-in-a-drawer' scent worn by Janice. It had reminded me of something, sometime in the past. School days? No, another time - one that had been exciting although not entirely happy. After a while I remembered: it was that first year at university. The Saturday dances! All those girls!

It was getting on towards evening. I walked to the kitchen, mixed myself a gin and tonic and carried it back to the garden. I thought again of that year in the mid-1950s. On Saturday nights, Dennis and I would go down to the pub - or just to a coffee bar if we were hard up - and stay there until about 8.00; and then we'd go on to the 'college hop'.

My last contact with Dennis had been seven years before, when I had written to tell him that Margaret had died. Before that, we hadn't really communicated much beyond exchanging Christmas cards every year; and even that stopped when I lost Maggie - she being the one to do the cards and that sort of thing. I suddenly felt like making contact again.

It took a while. First I discovered that I had no email address for him so I phoned. The number I tried was not recognised; and further enquiry revealed he was ex-directory. In the end I sent a post-card - one of my own photographs of the salt marsh plants. After carefully setting out my house address, email address and phone number I just had room to squeeze in:

> It's been a long time. Hope you are well.
> I shall be in Liverpool last week in Sep.
> Thought of visiting you on way home.
> Let me know if possible/convenient.
> Look forward to hearing. Mike Rowe

On the way to and from the post-box I continued reminiscing. Conditioned no doubt by school and university, I have long felt that the year starts in the autumn; and my memory of that particular September had an almost mythical sense of beginnings about it. Not unusual, I suppose. Countless other people must have similar memories and feelings for their time at university - especially for the start. The corny old phrase 'the happiest days of your life' popped into my head. That was supposed to be your schooldays - not always a happy time for me. But, that first year at university - would I describe that as 'happy'?

2

The moment the train starts moving again, Mike turns to Dennis and says, "We're going the wrong way!"

Dennis merely shrugs, but one of the two male students sitting opposite them looks up and seems keen to explain: "We came into Shrewsbury from the Midlands." His right hand describes an arc in the air. "And now, another locomotive, coupled to the other end of the train, is pulling us out again - and round into Wales." His left hand describes another arc.

"You seem very knowledgeable," says Dennis. "Are you by any chance a train spotter?" He glances towards Mike, who quickly looks away to avoid colluding in any mockery.

The student grins. "Well, yes, I used to be, but I know this route pretty well by now - I've done it so many times."

"What are you studying?" asks Mike, keen to change the subject.

"Geology - I'm just about to start my honours year. I gather you two are freshers."

"That's right," replies Dennis. He stands up. "Please excuse me gentlemen - now that the train is moving again I'm going for a slash." He slides open the door and steps into the side corridor."

After a short silence, the student resumes by asking, "Why are you going up so late? You've missed Freshers' Week."

"Well," says Mike, "Dennis had to postpone going - family matters. And I didn't want to travel up on my own. We're from the same school." While Mike speaks he observes the fresh, youthful face of the student and thinks that he doesn't look old enough to be a third year.

The second student who has been reading and ignoring the conversation suddenly speaks up: "You may come to regret missing Freshers' Week."

"Why. . . why do you say that?"

This student is darker and bigger and looks as though he really could be a third year. He closes his book. "Well, you've missed a good chance of finding your way around. And," he smiles and raises his eyebrows in emphasis, "because that's when much of the pairing-off takes place. There's a shortage of women - you do realise that, don't you?" He re-opens his book and goes back to reading.

The first student begins telling Mike about the different societies and other activities he is involved with and how useful they are in getting to know people. Then, in response to a question from Mike, he goes on to describe in detail the geology field project that took up much of his summer vacation.

After a time, trying to follow the details, Mike finds his attention wandering. He notices that Dennis has come back but is remaining outside in the corridor. He would like to get away and join him, but has to wait for a suitably polite moment. While half-listening he has been looking sideways at Dennis's tall shape, slouching, his head slightly out of the window. The word 'nonchalant' comes to mind; and he remembers how he once looked up that word and found it originally meant 'lacking heat'. That's Dennis all right - sometimes he could be amusing, intelligent company but Mike hadn't taken to him during the early years at school. It was only in the second year Sixth Form that they had become friends.

Five minutes later the two of them are standing in the corridor on each side of the wooden carriage door, talking, speculating about the exciting immediate future. There is a waft of warm, smoky, sulphurous air from the open window. Dennis wrinkles his long nose and goes to close the window. Mike thinks of saying that he enjoys railway smells and their associations, but decides not to.

Some time later they have solved two immediate problems: finding *Ty Glas*, their boarding house, and then getting their luggage transported there. Now they can relax. Their landlady, Mrs Griffiths, serves up a hot meal and a short list of house rules. They dine on their own. She explains that the other two men in the digs, both second years - she calls them 'boys' - are out at the moment. The dining room is illuminated by a central light, filtered and fogged by a yellow, marbled, glass bowl lampshade. The furniture - chairs, table, sideboard and fire-surround - are of yellowish oak. After they finish eating they, too, are eager to go out.

It has been dark for some time and they are exploring the town centre. Along one street they are met by a blast of moist sea air. Mike remarks on its fresh sweet qualities - different, it seems to him, from the cockle, mud and weed smells of his familiar bit of Essex coast. Minutes later they are walking along the promenade, dodging huge waves that are striking the sea wall and sending up spray into the darkness. They turn into another street and are met by groups of students, some whooping and shouting, some singing. At the far end is a war-memorial around which many more are gathered. The songs are an odd mixture - some are recognised by Mike as the rugby kind, others are quaint, old-fashioned things. One goes 'When we leave this bloody college. . .' to the same tune as 'When this bloody war is over. . .'

3

"Mike! Good to see you. You managed to find us then, without any help."

"Well. . . not quite. I made two attempts to call you on the mobile but no signal - I had to ask at the village shop. One day I shall get around to buying a sat-nav."

Before entering I glanced at the cottage. It seemed of indeterminate size, merging as it did with various outbuildings. I ducked my head under the stone lintel and followed Dennis through a hall and then into a kitchen. It was warm and spacious, and equipped with a pine table and chairs, a Welsh dresser and an Aga.

I sat at the table and observed Dennis as he made tea from the kettle that sat on the stove. He hadn't changed much - his thin face remained quite youthful for a man coming up to seventy - but he didn't seem as tall as I remembered, even allowing for a rather pronounced stoop.

"Well," he said, as soon as he'd sat down, "I wouldn't describe this as being 'on your way home' from Liverpool to Devon. Do you normally travel by such devious routes?"

I felt a bit foolish - my decision to arrange the visit had been sudden and groundless, just a whim. Eventually I replied "I didn't mind going out of my way - it's a long time since I saw this part of Wales."

We went on to exchange news of what we were currently doing. He told me of his and Gwen's involvement with local operatic and drama groups. Later, when I mentioned my natural history and photography activities, he spoke of his recently revived interest in drawing and painting. I remembered his skill in drawing - it seemed to go with his enthusiasm for zoology - but he explained how he now appreciated colour as much as form. I told him more of my interest in marine ecology; and I reminded him that at school, and as an undergraduate, his passion had been for fishes - keeping them, studying them, catching them. Was he still an angler? No, but he was still keen on aquatic things. That prompted him to reiterate - I knew much of it already - how, after getting his degree in zoology, he had gone up to Scotland to do research on salmon. Following that, he trained to be a teacher and had remained in the profession until he retired. Unlike me, he had avoided National Service.

We went on to exchange more about work and retirement. While we talked I had been gaining the impression that we were the only two in the house. It felt impolite to ask where Gwen was so I asked, "How's Gwen?"

"She's OK. She's away at the moment - visiting her sister in Dolgellau. She'll be back tomorrow."

Later that afternoon we went for a long walk, through the village and then up a steep hill from where we could see the mountains of Snowdonia, grey against a bright, yellowish sky in the west. On the way back I picked up a piece of rock that had caught my attention, having traces of what looked like fossils in it. "What are we on here - is it Cambrian?"

"Ordovician, I think."

I tried to get him to talk more about geology but he showed no interest. He talked instead of people from our old school and their various fortunes - people I hadn't thought about since we both went up to university in autumn 1956. I wasn't surprised to hear that he had kept in touch with his old fishing buddy Alan, but he seemed to know a lot about others, hardly known to me in those days. Then he explained: both he and Gwen had been contacting people from their old schools via the internet.

We got back to the cottage at about 6.00 and, after changing our footwear, we walked in the other direction to a pub, the *Carreg Hogi*, where we had a couple of pints and a meal. We talked about our children, their marriages, their lives and their problems; and then about our grandchildren and their schools, and our misgivings concerning state education in England and Wales since the 1980s.

We walked back along the lane to the cottage in almost complete darkness. Once inside, we sat by the stove and finished the evening with coffee and more reminiscence before he showed me to my bedroom.

Just before falling asleep I remembered that Gwen would be returning tomorrow. I found I could picture quite clearly the way she had looked, nearly fifty years ago. Since that time I hadn't even seen a photo of her. I amused myself by trying to imagine in what ways she might have changed.

4

A bright morning, at the beginning of November. Mike is sitting in the dining room at *Ty Glas* enjoying the fact that he can linger over breakfast, not having a nine o'clock lecture that day. Sitting opposite him is the bulky blonde figure of Huw.

The door opens and Dennis's head appears round it. "Listen," he says, "I've just heard some more news on the radio about the Suez situation." He pauses before continuing: "All National Service deferment is to be reviewed. So, it looks as though we'll all be going off to Egypt together!"

Next moment there is a scuffle and Dennis is pitched into the room, followed by Gareth who has obviously pushed him.

"Don't take any notice!" shouts Gareth. "That's not what they said on the news. He's making it up - I heard him practising upstairs, getting the words right."

"You spoiler!" says Dennis.

Mike experiences an odd hiatus before things begin to happen. There is a binding feeling in the gut, a wave of prickling that goes along his arms to the backs of his hands, then a sense of weakness and dread.

Suddenly there is Huw, pushing back his chair, lurching to a standing position, and lunging towards their tormentor shouting "You bastard!" Dennis dodges and avoids contact.

Gareth - looking dark and diminutive between the opponents - manages to keep them apart until Huw calms down. During this time Mike attempts to carry on eating. Eventually it is safe for Dennis, before he exits by the front door, to deliver a brief explanation: "It was envy. You three haven't got niners this morning - I have. I felt like stirring things up, doing a bit of mischief."

Throughout the day - at lectures in the morning when attention drifts, and in the afternoon in the chemistry laboratories, while waiting for things to filter - Mike recalls that breakfast-time event. The first response each time is a touch of fear - it had begun to occur to him that there might be some truth behind the story, something Dennis actually did hear on the radio. He remembers that Huw had recently told them of the Government's plans to call up reserves, including *ex*-National Servicemen like his brother. This leads Mike to speculate grimly about further developments. The Suez crisis has penetrated through his general lack of concern about politics and the outside world. It is now something to be worried about. Dread of National Service is bad enough but Suez brings to mind those fearful things the adults used to talk about when he was a child: the Berlin blockade; the menace of the Soviet Union; the seeming inevitability of a third world war - an atomic war. Occasionally he feels a bit of amusement because he likes hoaxes, as long as people don't get hurt. Dennis really shouldn't have done that, though - maybe there'll be an opportunity for revenge another day.

It is in the evening of the day after the hoax that Dennis drops his second bombshell. Mike and Gareth walk back to *Ty Glas* after sitting hopefully over cups of frothy coffee in the cafe on the corner - the one where female students are sometimes to be found. Dennis would normally have been with them but, after supper, he had announced mysteriously that he had something else to do that evening.

As they enter the front door, they are met by an agitated Huw. "You can't go in there!" he declares, pointing to the parlour door. "He's got a bloody woman in there!"

At a loss to know what to do, they follow Huw up to his room where he explains that Dennis had suddenly arrived, at about 9.30, ". . .with a bloody woman in tow" and had taken her into the parlour. After a short introduction Huw had felt that his presence wasn't wanted.

"He can't do that," complains Gareth. "He can't keep us out - it's our home, isn't it. I'm going in." But he makes no move as yet; and the three look at each other in silence - Huw, glowering, sitting on the single chair, Mike and Gareth sitting on the bed.

"So," observes Gareth, "that's the reason he didn't come out tonight - had a date, isn't it? Do you know anything about her? Is she town or college?" Huw shrugs. Gareth continues: "If she's a col' girl she could be in trouble - they're not supposed to visit men in their digs."

"And it's nearly 11.00," says Mike. "She'll have to get back to her hall of residence." Gareth suddenly stands up. "I'm going in." A few minutes later he returns, grinning. "She *is* a col' girl! I don't know her name - she's a fresher - but I've seen her in the Geog. Department."

"What did you do?" asks Mike, "just walk in? I didn't hear you knock."

"Oh yes. I pretended to be surprised, of course, and I apologised for disturbing them."

"There's brave!" says Huw, beginning to look amused at last. "Did you catch them at it?"

Gareth laughs. "No, nothing like that. Still got their coats on! We talked for a bit and then I came straight back to report."

Mike stands up. "Come on, let's go and join them."

After they are introduced, the main mystery becomes resolved. Gwen is a student - but she is also a town girl. She lives with her parents, not far from *Ty Glas*, in fact. She doesn't see how any rule about female students not visiting men in their lodgings can apply to her: her mother knows Mrs Griffiths - slightly - so she could be just visiting.

Huw's attitude has mellowed - he offers to go and make the tea and when he returns he actually pours Gwen a cup. He even offers her one of his mother's Welsh cakes.

Mike learns that she is studying 'jog jol 'n econ', a phrase he is now familiar with and knows to mean the popular combination of geography, geology and economics. Dennis also does geology, along with zoology and botany, and that's how they met. Lucky old Dennis!

As they converse, Mike observes Gwen, entertained by her lively personality and liking the way she looks. Her curvy figure is framed by her bulky navy-blue duffel coat. Draped around her shoulders like a stole is a university scarf - dark blue, maroon and gold. Her bobbed hair is thick and black; and her eyes, somehow both narrowed and expressive as she talks, remind him of the film star Gene Tierney. Lucky old Dennis. Lucky bastard!

§

5

The following morning over breakfast, Dennis spoke about his wife's return in the evening and revealed for the first time that he had to drive to Dolgellau to collect her. Gwen used to drive herself, he explained - still did if necessary - but preferred not to these days. Guessing there were no other plans for the day I proposed going in the morning - perhaps we could visit nearby Cadair Idris before collecting her.

In the middle of a grey afternoon we were sitting on a rock overlooking the mountain's crater-like lake. The surface of the water was very still. We had just finished our sandwiches and Dennis was having a cigarette. I had been surprised, the previous day, to find that he still smoked. We'd all smoked in those days - all except Huw who had tried to keep fit for the sake of his rugby, although he used to drink too much beer. But none of my present friends and acquaintances still smoked.

I picked up a stone and asked, "Is this Ordovician?"

He shrugged. "Possibly. I don't know. I seem to remember that Cadair is quite mixed."

"You used to be keen on geology, back then." He made no reply and I continued: "I remember going around with you one Saturday afternoon, while you measured the dip and strike of different rock exposures.

He looked up. "I think it's beginning to rain - we'd better get a move on."

It wasn't until the evening, back at the cottage, that I really looked at Gwen. My first sight of her by the car had been brief and what had struck me at the time was the sound of her voice - it was just as I remembered it. But I'd hardly seen her - all the way home she had sat behind me in the car.

The first thing I noticed was that her hair was still rather dark. Where she was grey, it resembled unpolished silver, or pewter. Her face had aged to the extent that I had imagined and, like the rest of her, was more plump and rounded.

After supper, they refused my offer to help with washing up and left me to sit in an armchair by the fire. I closed my eyes, risking falling asleep, and thought about the chain of chance events that had brought me there. Earlier, over the meal, we had talked about the courses our lives had taken. I expanded on the story of my sudden out-of-the-blue impulse to contact them. They followed by telling me about their contacting old friends from school and college through the internet. Names then emerged from the past - the 'deep past' as I had begun to think of it, with its aura of strangeness. I was reminded of dreams I had been having recently of school and university, dreams in which the architecture, the landscapes and the people were interestingly transformed.

Later, they came and sat with me by the fire. We talked more of this urge to contact the past; and I raised the question of whether it was a common symptom of old age. Dennis seemed to have a ready-made answer. He spoke of Erik Erikson, the psychoanalyst who wrote about the 'eight ages of man'. "Each age," explained Dennis, "is supposed to have its own particular conflict from which we learn - or fail - to grow. The last age - where we three are now - is about what Erikson called 'integrity versus despair'. It's the time when we struggle to give our lives meaning. . . I think it's got something to do with that."

Gwen pulled a face of exaggerated amazement. "Where did all that come from?" Dennis shrugged and grinned. "Someone from school I've been exchanging emails with."

They began talking more of old friends when Gwen, with a mischievous little smile, turned to me and said "One of our contacts from my old school is. . ." She raised her eyebrows. "A certain person - can you guess who?"

"No?" I waited for the answer.

She persisted: "Someone you knew, back in your college days?"

"Who's this?" asked Dennis.

"You know - she sent me that photo last week."

"Oh, you mean Mrs Casaubon."

"Yes." She turned to me again. "I'm talking about Linda! - Linda Thomas, as she was back then."

Linda. My feelings were put on hold as Gwen told me more, some of which was already known but forgotten - such as the fact that Linda had gone on to marry John Price, a postgraduate student, and that they had gone to live somewhere in the Midlands where he worked as a university lecturer.

Then, going beyond what I knew, she talked of recently contacting Linda, and of learning that her husband had died in 1990.

"And Linda married again" I put in, stating what seemed the obvious.

"Oh no, she's not married."

I glanced at Dennis. "Didn't you refer to her as 'Mrs Casaubon'?

"That was just his little joke," Gwen explained. "Have you read Middlemarch?"

"Yes, I thought I recognised the name from somewhere. What's the connection?"

"Well, I expect you remember: the heroine, Dorothea Brooke, marries this old clergyman scholar; and she's all set to devote her life to helping him write his great book - his *magnum opus*, isn't it? - but it never gets finished. Well, Linda ended up like that. She got involved with this man - much older than her, he was - and spent years working as his unpaid secretary. . ."

"And unpaid editor and unpaid researcher, from what I hear," put in Dennis.

"Were they. . . are they. . . in a relationship?" I asked.

"I haven't been able to glean that," said Gwen, with a grin. "But she's definitely finished with him now, so she tells me."

At that point the telephone rang and Gwen spent nearly half an hour talking to the caller. I wanted to hear more about Linda so I tried to keep the conversation going. But Dennis knew very little and, by the time Gwen returned, she was occupied with other matters and wanted to call it a night.

Before going to sleep, thinking back, I mused on how misleading memory can be when it comes to the duration of periods and events. I now realised that that exciting time when Dennis and I had gone about together - to cafes and dances, hoping to meet girls - had only lasted a single month. As soon as he got to know Gwen, he spent most of his spare time with her, leaving me to go out on my own, or with other friends such as Gareth. For me that was the start of a much longer period - a time of frustration. Until I met Linda.

§

6

Breakfast time on a cold grey morning - a time between Rag Week and the Easter Vacation. Mike is explaining why he sometimes has his midday meal in one of the restaurants in town rather than the refectory:

"Well, it's very cheap - if you have the set lunch, that is - and it makes a change."

"But what is wrong with the refectory?" asks Gareth.

"He is avoiding the *re-faectory*," puts in Dennis, "because that's where the rabbits dine at night." He is ignored - they've all heard the joke before.

Mike eventually admits that he sometimes feels like eating away from other students. "You're just anti-social," mumbles Huw.

Midday. Mike's morning has included a chemistry lecture and a visit to the post-office. He arrives at the restaurant and is met by welcome heat and familiar smells. The place is crowded, giving the impression of no available seats, and he wonders if he will have to go elsewhere. Then he spots a place on the far side, near the window - a small table for two, occupied by a lone woman.

"Is this place free?"

She looks up. "Yes." She returns to eating and to reading. Her book is propped open by the flat rim of the dinner plate. It looks precarious.

After giving his order to the waitress he continues observing his companion. She is younger than she looked from a distance. Something about her appearance had the effect of ageing her - her permed hair, perhaps, or the rather formal suit with its fitted jacket and lapels. She turns a page and tries to tuck it under the edge of the plate. The attempt fails, previous pages flick back, and she loses her place.

"It's frustrating when that happens, isn't it," says Mike, stopping himself from going on about bindings and elastic recoil.

She smiles, revealing a little gap between her front teeth. "Serves me right for reading at table." Nice voice. She closes her book, puts it in a bag by her feet and gets on with her meal.

He now sees her as a girl rather than a woman and wonders about her age. He wants to start a conversation but, unable to think of an opener, decides it's better not to intrude just yet - he'll wait till she's finished eating.

He looks around, wondering how long he will have to wait before his meal arrives. He is about to say something when she suddenly pushes back her chair. What a shame! - she's finished and about to leave - he's missed his chance of getting to know her. But no, he hasn't - she's only standing up to reach for her bag and take out her cigarettes.

"You don't mind if I smoke, do you?"

"No, not at all." He wishes he had a lighter he could flourish; but he's only got matches - and they're in his coat pocket, hanging by the door. Unable to think of anything else to say he asks, "Are you a student?"

"No - I'm a town girl." There is a suggestion of a knowing smile.

"Well, you could be both," he says; "I know someone who's both. You might know her. She's a fresher - a first year. Gwen Daniels?"

It turns out that she does know Gwen - slightly. They were both at the grammar school, although she was two years behind Gwen. Which means two years younger than him, seventeen, or thereabouts. In the ensuing conversation he talks about himself - too much, he later worries - and gets to learn that her name is Linda, that she left school after getting her O Levels, and that she works in an office in the *neuadd y dref* - the Town Hall.

Just as she is about to leave, he asks the question he has been silently rehearsing: would she like to go out with him the following Saturday to see a film? To his delight and relief she says yes; and they arrange a time to meet outside the cinema.

As soon as she has gone his food arrives. It resembles the set meal of previous days: meat and gravy with peas, a wedge of Yorkshire pudding, and domes of mashed potato and pale cabbage - obviously dispensed with an ice-cream scoop, just as they used to be at school dinners.

§

7

It was sometime after 8.00pm and we were sitting round a table in the *Carreg Hogi*, waiting for the last course to arrive.

"It seems to have got dark very early," remarked Gwen.

I agreed. The day had been such a hot, bright one and the evening air smelt and felt more like early August than late September.

Dennis began talking about other people who had been at university with us. I only recognised one or two names although other individuals came to mind when described or put into context.

Gwen suddenly asked me: "Would you like to meet up with Linda again?"

During the day, being driven through West Wales - my 'blue remembered hills' - many things had reminded me of Linda; but I'd resisted the temptation to ask any further questions, or even to mention her name. "No," I replied. "I don't think so. It wouldn't be a good idea."

She leaned towards me and said, with a sort of conspiratorial emphasis, "You two were very keen back then, I remember - couldn't keep your hands off each other!"

This made me laugh. "Well, yes - back then - but I don't think she'd want anything to do with me now."

Our conversation turned to the present. They told me about their amateur drama activities and of the choral society and the madrigal group to which they belonged. It brought back to me that these and all things to do with music and singing had been Gwen's concerns in the past. One of the things I remembered about her was her trying to persuade

Dennis to go to a local singing event - a *gymanfa ganu* - I even recalled the name for it. I was amused about the changes in Dennis. It wasn't just the singing - in those days you couldn't have found anyone more English and less Welsh than he.

Back at the house, over coffee, we talked about our travels of the day and Dennis asked me "Where would you like to go tomorrow?"

"I haven't thought about it. Is there anywhere you've got in mind - somewhere you'd like to go yourself?"

It was Gwen who replied, eagerly: "Well now, you've had your pilgrimage to the west, to the coast. How would you like to go in the other direction?"

Dennis turned to her. "Where have you got in mind?"

"I was a thinking of Shrewsbury - haven't been there for a while. I could do some shopping while you two boys went off and did your own thing."

Shrewsbury turned out to be a good choice. So far, I had been unsuccessful in getting Dennis to talk about geology. To him, it was just something he had studied in his first year and then dropped. However, he was happy to go along with my recent interest in palaeontology; and he offered to take me to one or two fossiliferous sites he used to know that might still be accessible. So, having spent a little time in the town, we left Gwen to her shopping and drove south along the A49 towards Church Stretton.

He seemed puzzled about my interest. I told him how it had developed only lately - from my marine ecology work. I reminded him of the fact that I hadn't studied the subject back at university - that my three first-year subjects had been chemistry, physics and maths.

Our searches were disappointing. The first site no longer existed and the second was now a weedy, sad-looking, unofficial tip, although it did produce a few fragments. We looked around the area for any new rock exposures before calling it a day. Before going back to Shrewsbury I took some photographs of the Longmynd, partly because it looked so beautiful and more colourful than I remembered, and partly because I now held it in awe, knowing it to be of pre-cambrian age.

On meeting up with Gwen again I proposed getting some afternoon tea in a cafe before we set out for home. But the suggestion was ignored. My two friends had gone rather quiet; and, as we drove out of the town centre, I had a growing feeling that there was something going on. The mystery didn't resolve until we had just left Shrewsbury and were heading back west.

Dennis suddenly said, with good-humoured impatience, "Come on - you'll have to tell him - we're nearly there!"

"Oh. . . yes. . . Can you find somewhere to stop for a minute?"

After the car had come to a halt, she explained what had been planned:

Linda, it was disclosed, lived near Shrewsbury, quite close to where we had stopped. Gwen had got it into her head the night before that we ought to meet. The fact that I'd said I wasn't interested had not discouraged her. In the morning, she had phoned Linda to tell her that she and Dennis would be in Shrewsbury, and would it be all right to call in on the way home, time permitting? Having been assured of their welcome she'd phoned again, a little later, to reveal that Mike Rowe, that student from her past, was staying with them. How would she feel about them bringing him along? And it seemed that Linda had agreed.

So, I reflected, Gwen shared Dennis's propensity for dropping bombshells. I couldn't reply at first - I was aware of a feeling resembling panic. Eventually I said, with more feeling in my voice than I intended, "You shouldn't have done that! You must have really put her on the spot! And, how is it going to look if I refuse? I *am* going to refuse! You know, when we parted there was a lot of animosity. . ."

"It's all right!" She brandished her mobile at me. "I've given you a get-out. Don't forget - I said 'time permitting'. I'll just call and say we don't have time after all." She paused. "Are you sure you don't want to see her?"

"Yes, I am sure!"

She made the call. It gave me an odd feeling - she was actually talking to Linda. Linda, from all those years ago, was there, replying, even though I couldn't hear her voice.

Before I set out for Devon the next morning, Gwen reproached me in a good-natured way for being such a coward. I was in the mood to agree, to the extent that I accepted her offer of Linda's address and said that I *might*, at some point, if and when I was ready, write to her.

8

A pile of mail had accumulated on my doormat while I had been away over Christmas but the moment I glanced at the envelope I knew that the card was from her. The post-mark was completely illegible so it must have been the writing although I had no conscious recollection of what Linda's writing looked like.

A week or so before, I had sent her a Christmas card; and along with a short message I had included my land line number and my address. And it actually got posted - unlike the letter I had started, following my trip to Wales, but abandoned after several re-writes.

I stared at the winter scene on the card for a second or two before looking inside. Beneath the printed greeting was her own expression of wishes for the season followed by 'Linda' written in a distinctive way that I did remember. And there was her telephone number.

I put off phoning her until one evening shortly after New Year. I settled myself in a comfortable chair, a glass of something alcoholic to hand, and waited until enough courage had gathered to enable me to pick up the phone and enter the numbers. The answer came - a statement of the last three digits in a voice that could have belonged to anyone.

"Linda? Mike - Mike Rowe. Is this a convenient time to talk?"

"Yes - but let me phone you back - I get free calls after six."

It was a minute and a half before it rang. During the wait I replayed her voice in my head while searching my memory for comparison. There was some familiarity - a trace of her

Welsh accent - never strong. I recalled that her father had been Welsh but her mother English.

"I didn't recognise your voice," was the first thing I said on picking up the phone. "Did you recognise mine?"

"I'm not sure, but I guessed it was you."

My hand was shaking. If only she would say something else. I continued: "Do I still have the same Essex-cockney accent? That's what you used to say about me."

"A bit, but your voice has changed - it's deeper." I wanted to get away from this topic but could think of nothing to say in reply. She went on, eventually: "I was sorry to hear that your wife had died."

"I was sorry to hear about John."

And so it proceeded for nearly an hour. We spoke of our children: her two girls and my two girls. We said a little about our late partners, the things they liked, the things they did, the tragedy of their illnesses and subsequent deaths.

It all seemed unsatisfactory. As we finished I couldn't help commenting on the way I felt. "Our conversation - it hasn't really got off the ground, has it?"

"I wondered about that myself," she replied. "But I thought of a reason - all the time we knew each other back then, we hardly ever talked on the telephone. It was all face to face, or letters."

"I suppose that could be it," I said, glad she'd understood my comment. "Linda. . . I'd like to come and visit you. We could talk properly! What do you think?"

A pause, then: "We'll see. I'll phone you tomorrow - about this time, if that's ok."

§

9

I don't like driving as much as I did when I was younger, so being able to travel by train on this occasion was a treat, something to be savoured.

It was early February and I was staying with my younger daughter, Lucy, in Birmingham - something I often did around New Year time if I had not spent Christmas with her. Before going there I told her about Linda, simply describing her as 'an old girl-friend from my college days'; and it had been Lucy's welcome suggestion that while I was there I could take a trip to Shrewsbury - being so close - and call on her. So I was now enjoying a train ride, a window seat and the excitement and anticipation of seeing Linda for the first time since making contact.

Half an hour to go. I thought of using the time to do some serious thinking - maybe plans to do with my conservation work. I closed my eyes. Soon, however, the rhythms and comforts of the train were evoking thinking of a different kind - more the stream of consciousness type.

A chain of associations led me to recall the time immediately after Maggie's sudden death. This was not one of my melancholic Maggie moments; I was reviewing the memory in a detached way - not feeling the emotions, just recalling the strange states of mind I had experienced. There had been a kind of shift in my perception of reality, of the actual physical world. I remembered thinking that even clouds seemed different and, I felt, would never look the same again. Along with that had came the dying of all interest in the things we had been enjoying together after the children had left home such as rambling, gardening, architecture, antique fairs. At the same time there arose a split in the way I saw my own personal history: there was the time before I met Margaret and the time after. Pleasant things from the pre-Margaret times of childhood, youth and young adulthood remained untouched. But everything since then felt blighted. Even our important memories - now that they were solely mine, no longer shared, had become no better than fantasies, their authenticity sometimes cast into doubt. Part of my recovery had been to realise the obvious: that there was an equally rich store of memories still shared with my children and others. If only I had taken more account of them.

I looked out of the window and was surprised at the change in the landscape since I set out. The fields were being replaced by huge expanses of water. Bare winter trees, singly or in rows, floated on lakes or arose from little islands. Of course - the recent floods. Linda had described the plight of some of her friends, while assuring me she had not been affected.

Linda. Throughout the decades of my married life she had almost never come to mind - she could have been anywhere, dead or alive. But she had continued to exist - living, growing, changing, raising children, during all the Margaret years. I just couldn't think of them together, their two existences seemed. . . 'incongruent' was the word. Parallel universes. And equally incongruent, I felt convinced, were the Lindas of 1957 and 2007. Is that because the Linda of 2007 is real, while the Linda of 1957 has become mythologised?

I tried to remember the way she looked.

It is midday Friday, the day before the first date. Mike is walking along the sea front when he sees Linda coming towards him. He feels alarmed. Surprised by this response, he reacts against it by quickening his pace towards her.

They exchange words of greeting.

He finishes with "Six-thirty tomorrow then?" instantly anxious at having made it a question.

"Yes," she replies, "see you tomorrow."

They part. It is a bright day and he has been noticing things. There was a shy quality to her smile and he finds the little gap in her teeth very attractive. Her height is about five feet four inches to his five feet nine - just right. Her eyes are brown and her short hair is not black as he had supposed but dark chestnut.

The passengers blocking my way seemed to be unnecessarily slow in getting off the train and I was feeling frustrated. I tried to exercise patience while I glanced out of the window every now and then, hoping to recognise her in the crowd on the platform.

I thought back to scenes like this when I had been the one standing on a platform, waiting for someone to emerge from a train. You always had to wait - they never seemed to be the first to alight - more likely the last. I tried to visualise such an actual occasion but all I got was the scene from the film *The Railway Children* where, after much agonised looking, there is still no sign of the awaited father - then, there he is, as if he has materialised, ghost-like, from the smoke.

I walked up and down the platform while it rapidly emptied. Who, or what, exactly was I looking for? I no longer had any photographs - just my memory images; and it was these that I had tried to age realistically. During our last phone-call she had said "Don't expect me to look the way I used to - look out for a little old lady!" But there seemed to be no-one who fitted both my search image and that description.

"Mike?"

At my side was a woman - one I had actually half-noticed earlier in my search.

"Linda?"

I turned to face her properly. It was impossible. As I stared, my memories and constructions dissolved.

"Have I changed that much?"

"No, you *haven't*!" I replied, eventually.

10

We sat facing each other across a little table in a corner of a restaurant, just as we did when we first met. I gazed at her, attending with ease and interest to what she was saying, but acutely aware of her appearance - and the way it seemed to change. Whenever I looked away, to order something for example, I would turn back to find that she was even more recognisable as the girl I used to know.

It felt a bit crass but I couldn't resist commenting: "You look fantastic! Your hair - it's nearly the same colour!"

She smiled, in just the way I remembered. "Amazing what you can do, with the right chemicals."

I could only reply, redundantly, "Mine's completely white now."

After pouring the wine I began to ask about her life story from the time we broke up. She was reluctant at first and persuaded me to start with mine.

"Well, after I was demobbed I lived at home with my parents for about two years. I didn't know what I wanted to do with my life. I was trying to write science fiction. Do you remember - I'd started doing that after I was posted to Germany? I even harboured youthful hopes of making a career out of it but it wasn't to be - the market was changing and my plots and style were behind the times. Anyway, I tried various jobs during that time, and finally I found one in Bedfordshire that was just right for me."

"When did you go back to university, then?"

"I didn't. I didn't think they'd have me! As you'll remember only too well, I made a complete mess of things at the end of that first year - failed all my exams and had to leave, didn't I." I stopped at that point, smarting again, recalling the scorn and reproach I had discerned coming from parents, friends and from myself.

"But when we first talked on the phone you mentioned having a degree."

"Yes, I'm coming to that. While I was working I studied for an external London University degree. That was by going to college in the evenings, and on day release from work. It took longer to get it that way, but it was good for me - it meant I had to work harder."

"And when did you meet Margaret?"

"Your turn," I suggested. "Let me hear your story - from the time we parted." She said nothing for a while and so I prompted: "That was in 1959."

"Yes. During the long, hot summer. It was a wonderful summer, wasn't it - do you remember?"

"I remember it," I replied, "but I didn't like it! It seemed to go on for ever."

"I'm sorry!"

I shrugged and tried to sound breezy. "Tell me about getting to know John. I never knew him, except by sight."

"It was in the autumn."

Something occurred to me. "Did you know him before we broke up?"

She smiled. "No, don't worry, you didn't overlap. We met in October - the start of the college year."

"He was a few years older than you, wasn't he?"

"Well he was 25 - and I was just about to be 20. He'd got his degree that summer - in philosophy - and he was going for a Ph.D."

"When did you get married?"

"A year later - as soon as I was 21."

"That was quick!"

"Well, we fell for each other; and there was no point in hanging about. Hayley came along two years later."

"She'll be in her 40s now," I mused, thinking of my own daughters. "Where does she live? I think you told me but I've forgotten."

"Cardiff. She and her husband are GPs."

"And your second daughter. . . Sarah?

"Born seven years later. She lives down your way - in Exeter."

The food arrived at that point. After we had settled to eating she continued, "Your turn now - tell me about Margaret."

I related how Maggie and I had met in Bedford in the autumn of 1961, when I moved there to take up the job. We were living in flats in the same building. The previous talk of the summer of 1959 led me by contrast to go on about the terrible winter of 1962-3 - the power-cuts, the permanently frozen plumbing, the shared misery that afflicted Maggie and me and probably bonded us together. "I think struggle was the secret of the success of our marriage. We started with nothing and neither of us was earning much. We spent years being hard up. And we built up our lives together."

"It was much the same for us at first," said Linda. "I didn't earn a lot and John's grant was only barely adequate."

We went on in this vein, throughout the meal, exchanging little stories about the early years with our partners.

Afterwards, we walked the short distance back to Linda's house, she holding my arm formally.

She showed me into a large sitting/dining room, turned on the gas fire, and insisted I make myself comfortable while she went to make coffee in the kitchen. I looked at the room from where I sat in one of the two armchairs by the fire. All around were family photographs - on walls, sideboard and shelves. John was recognisable; and I surmised that the two gowned and mortar-boarded young women were their daughters on their graduation days. A few minutes later she returned carrying a tray with coffee cups and, after placing it on a small table, sat down on the other armchair, half facing me.

After we had sat in silence for a while I finished my coffee and put the cup down. Now seemed like a good moment to own up. "That time when I was staying with Gwen and Dennis - when Gwen told you they were bringing me to see you - how did you feel about it?"

"Very strange."

"You know, we could easily have found time to call on you that day. But I refused - I panicked. Gwen had arranged the visit without my knowing - and I chickened out!"

The look she gave me was hard to interpret. I thought I had caused offence, but then realised she was puzzled, not hurt. Her response was a simple "Why?"

"Misgivings. . . all that unhappiness. I still feel guilty about those days."

"Why? - they weren't that bad." She smiled again. "We were very young and we just weren't right for each other. Anyway, I was the one who broke off our unofficial engagement. What do you feel guilty about?"

"Well, I caused all that acrimony, the conflict between you and your family. You ran away from home because of me."

She reached across and gently placed her hand on mine. "That would have happened inevitably - at some point. You helped me to make the break - and I'm grateful for that.

I was beginning to find the fire uncomfortably hot. She picked up on this and said "Are you too warm here?"

"A bit," I replied.

She turned the fire down and said "Come and sit on the sofa."

As soon as I had settled there next to her she continued, "If I hadn't left home when I did, I wouldn't have got to know John - so I'm grateful for that as well."

I struggled to reply, the words catching in my throat. "It's nice of you to say that but I know what I was like in those days: shallow. . . pathetic. . . feckless. . . a big let-down."

"You weren't 'feckless'! *Reckless* maybe. All those things you got up to during your National Service! I remember the lengths you went to, to get away, to be with me."

"Oh yes - those short, painful leaves."

She took my hand. "It wasn't just official leave though, was it? There was a bit of French leave as well. I remember my reckless young soldier going AWOL just to be with me - and being found out, and marched off 'under escort' as you put it in your letter!"

"Only the once! Mostly it was those 36 hour or 48 hour passes, whenever I could get one. And hitch-hiking, when I had no money for train fare."

"And you used to do other men's guard duties for cash, didn't you? Just so you could save up the fare." She continued, with a slight change in her voice: "You went without a lot of sleep in those days." She leaned towards me and gave me one of those mischievous looks that I remembered from the past. "But you never seemed short of energy!"

I had just begun to say something when I was interrupted by the telephone ringing in the hall. Linda went to answer it and came back a few minutes later, wearing an odd smile. "That was my neighbour, Dawn. She knew you were coming and she was worried about me. 'You may have known him once,' she said, 'but who knows how he's turned out? He might have become an axe-murderer.' She insisted on phoning to make sure I was all right!"

She sat down next to me again. I wanted to reply but, suddenly distracted by sheer awareness of her presence, I found I couldn't speak.

She responded to my silence by saying "I expect you're feeling tired after your journey. Shall we call it a night?"

"I'm not tired. . ." I began. But she had picked up the tray and was making her way to the kitchen. I guessed she wanted to bring the evening to a close.

In the morning there was a cold, silvery quality to the light outside and it seemed to set the agenda for our mood. We talked of ordinary, obvious things: her plans for the rest of the day which included afternoon tea with a friend and book club in the evening; my imminent train journey back to Lucy's home in Birmingham and my driving back to Devon three days later.

Shortly before departing I was in my room, gathering up the few things I had brought. I recalled, with distanced feelings at first, the previous evening with all its amazement. In the night, I had found it impossible to lie still in my bed. It was like Christmas when I was a child - unable to sleep until about 4am. Linda, my Linda, my very own Linda from the days of university, of National Service, of my misspent youth - was lying there, alive, breathing, just a few feet from me in the next room! It was time-travel - nothing less. Then Linda's voice brought me out of my reverie; it was time to go.

Sitting next to her as she drove me to the railway station in Shrewsbury, I found the courage and opportunity to ask one of two questions I had been holding in abeyance. "Linda. . . I was wondering. . . I'd normally go back from Birmingham to Devon along the M5. But, I could drive back this way, and then go down the A49. The Welsh Marches – I like that route. And, if it's all right with you, I could call on you again before going home. "

As I made my way onto the platform I was aware of a curious sense of well being, a feeling of being passively propelled along on a cushion of warm air. It was all arranged: I was going to visit Linda in three days time, spending two nights and a day with her before going home.

§

11

I woke suddenly, startled by the cacophony of the alarm signal from my mobile phone. After a moment of bewilderment I remembered where I was: at Lucy's home.

There had been a dream; the images, the people and the peculiar situation were dissolving rapidly, leaving only the feelings, and a sense of significance. I lay still for a while in the hope of recalling it; but I soon gave up. Then I remembered that earlier in the night I had woken from another much clearer dream - one in which Margaret had figured. I sometimes have dreams in which Margaret and I are engaged in some activity of an ordinary, happy kind. The girls are still with us; and we are all young. During the year following Maggie's death, she sometimes figured in another kind of dream - a lucid one. I would encounter her somewhere, or catch sight of her across a room, or through a window. I would feel great joy and surprise, and I would say something like "You've come back!" or "You've been gone such a long time!" Then I would get that "Oh, no - you're not really here!" feeling. In the early dreams I would physically hold on to her, trying to postpone the moment when I knew reality would take her away. In later ones I didn't get the chance - I just woke up as soon as I realised it was only a dream.

Why had I set the alarm? Of course - I'd planned to leave early. This arrangement was mainly for Lucy's benefit because she wanted me out of the house before she went off to work. But it suited me as well, because I wanted to get to Shrewsbury by midday; and Lucy's need helped me feel less guilty about my eagerness to get away.

Even though enjoying this visit to my daughter and her husband, my thoughts had been defaulting to Linda whenever I was on my own. Lucy had noticed this and had commented more than once that I seemed pre-occupied. Each time she said it I felt a little guilty, even though telling myself that guilt wasn't justified.

Linda opened the front door just as I reached it. After a kiss and a hug in the hallway she broke away saying "I'm in the middle of composing an awkward email. I won't be long. How about you going to the kitchen - make us some coffee?"

Having found the necessary items I did as she asked. When it was ready I waited for a minute or so, wondering if she intended to join me. Eventually I found a tray and went to look for her.

There she sat, working at her computer by the window - looking very graceful, just as she once used to sit at her huge typewriter in the town hall. I put the tray down on a table near the door and found myself a chair.

"I've nearly finished," she said, still typing swiftly.

The coffee was too hot to drink right away so I stood up to look at the bookshelves that covered two walls of the room. She stopped at that point and came over to the table.

"I was remembering how much you loved reading," I said. "You used to talk a lot about poetry and novels - English literature." I waved towards the mass of books on my left. I sat down again. "I used to think you might study for a degree in English one day. Did you ever. . . do anything in the way of higher education?"

"No. Many years ago my daughters talked me into taking A Levels at evening class but I didn't go any further. John was always urging me to do an Open University degree but I wasn't inclined - although the Arts Foundation Course looked interesting."

I stood up again and went over to study the spines and titles stacked against the other wall. Here were books on philosophy, psychology, anthropology, social and other sciences.

"Do you mind. . .? I asked. She waved her hand. I examined three or four of them. "John's, I suppose."

"Some are John's, some are mine."

Of course - the one in my hand had only been published three years before.

My unasked question came to mind. "There's something I've been wanting to ask you," I began: "Gwen told me about your working with someone on a book - a big project, I gather. Dennis referred to you as 'Mrs Casaubon." Linda made no response so I added, "You remember - Dorothea? - in *Middlemarch*?"

"Yes, I know. He wasn't the first to call me that." There was a clear lack of humour in the way she spoke.

"I'm sorry - is it something you don't want to talk about?"

She shrugged. "I don't mind."

"Is he famous - would I have heard of him?"

"I doubt it. Didn't Gwen tell you his name? It's Eric Vaughan." She looked thoughtful, slightly amused. "You know, there's more than one connection with George Eliot. Do you know anything about her partner, George Henry Lewes?"

"No?"

"Well, he was a writer himself - very talented, bit of a polymath. As well as plays and literary things, he wrote a lot on science. Well, towards the end of his life he was working on a big, all embracing study of psychology called 'Problems of Life and Mind'. And he wrote, in one of his letters, something about the shadow of old Casaubon hanging over him. He jokes about his great project as being a 'key to all psychologies' - referring, of course, to the '*Key to all Mythologies*' which was Casaubon's unfinished work. He goes on to say he's afraid he will have to leave it for Marian - that's George Eliot's real name - to finish. His own Dorothea."

"Mm. So, what was the subject of Eric Vaughan's book?"

"Psychology! It's a history of western psychology, from the ancient Greeks to the twentieth century."

"Well," I said, drinking the last of my coffee, "what a coincidence - if that's the right word. So, what happened - did George Eliot finish it?"

"Not in the way Casaubon had wanted. Lewes completed most of it himself before he died. Marian finished off Volumes Four and Five, and she made sure they were published."

"So, what happened about Eric's book?"

"He's still working on it as far as I know. I'm no longer involved."

"Will it ever be finished - and published?"

She shook her head sadly. "I don't think so. It's the way he works. Volume One was published. I worked hard on that with him, and I had to push him into completing it. As to the rest, I don't think it ever will be."

She looked away and gave the impression of not wanting to go on but I waited, saying nothing, hoping my silence would induce her into telling me more. Half a minute later I decided it wasn't going to work so I tried being more direct: "Tell me about Eric - if you don't mind, that is. How did you get to know him?"

She took a deep breath. "It was about three years after John died - that was in 1990. I'd been living here for a year or so when I was introduced to Eric. He'd retired and come to live nearby. He'd also been widowed a few years before. And we had other things in common, he having been an academic - he was a lecturer in psychology. As you know, John lectured in philosophy."

I wanted to find out more but, having only just arrived, it didn't seem the right time. I decided to leave it until later. The day having turned out to be a dry one, Linda suggested we might go out for a drive. We talked about it and decided to explore some parts of the borderlands that she liked and which were less familiar to me.

We started by driving towards Newtown. We had a light meal in an old but undistinguished pub and then headed first south-east and then north-east along Wenlock Edge to Much Wenlock. Travelling slowly and stopping every now and then to enjoy the view meant that the sun had set by the time we finally headed back towards Shrewsbury. I reflected that we had chosen the route fortuitously: travelling west in the morning and east in the afternoon meant that I wasn't dazzled so much by the horizon-hugging winter sun - something I find more bothersome, the older I get. Throughout the day we talked of people and places, holidays and children, sometimes about ourselves but almost never about our distant past.

It was completely dark when we arrived back in Shrewsbury. As soon as we were indoors I raised the subject of where we should go to eat that night. To my delight Linda explained that she had cooked our meal in advance and that it was just a matter of heating things up while we warmed ourselves.

Along with some red wine we got through the whole of the food - a substantial casserole of beef and vegetables - and finally finished off with coffee and a liqueur. This felt like the right time to ask:

"Linda. Have you. . . has there been anyone important in your life, since John?"

"Not in the way I think you mean."

"What about Eric - were you in any sort of relationship with him?"

She shook her head. "No. It might have gone that way. My life was so empty after John died. The girls had left home. Eric seemed such a. . . an admirable sort of man. Working with him was absorbing. . . worthwhile. . . it gave me a feeling of purpose."

"He was much older than you, wasn't he?"

"Eleven years - is that 'much older'?"

"Were you ever in love with him?" Before I had finished uttering it, the question was striking me as too blunt. "I hope you don't mind my asking. I need to know. . . I. . ."

"Why?"

"The answer is obvious, isn't it?"

"I don't know what you mean," she replied, with a mischievous look. "I need you to explain!"

I replied by taking her hand and kissing the back of her fingers. I had a new sense of being at one with myself - no more awkwardness. I turned her hand and pressed my lips to the palm.

Then we were lying, pressed tightly together on the sofa, laughing at the lack of space, the precariousness. That long kiss - our first proper, animated kiss - was an act of instant recognition, amazing familiarity.

At some point we parted spontaneously. Linda was the first to speak: "How can you carry on like this. . . with such an old lady?"

"She doesn't look or feel like an old lady - and she isn't acting like one."

She lowered her head, gazing upwards just as she used to, and said, "It feels. . . just like back then. I can't believe it's happening!"

We laughed when, changing position, I skilfully avoided falling off the sofa.

Shortly after midnight, I realised it was pointless trying to sleep and I switched on the bedside lamp and tried reading the book Lucy had lent me.

Some time later, on my way to the bathroom, I made sure to be as quiet as possible and not to switch on the landing light. As a result I was startled when I bumped into Linda on the way back.

"Hallo! I didn't wake you, did I?"

"No."

We stood there, in the dark, for a few seconds before I said, "I just can't sleep."

"Neither can I."

12

I didn't phone Linda until the morning after I got back home; and I immediately noticed a certain tone in the way she spoke, telling me something was wrong. Feelings were evoked of alarm, as though I expected a reproach - something from our past when reproach had figured much towards the end.

I asked what was wrong and instantly got the explanation. She was cross with me for not having phoned to say I had arrived home safely. She had been concerned about the weather forecast on the day I left. How *could* I forget to ring? So that was all it was. I apologised, trying not to betray my feelings of relief.

After we had finished, it dawned on me that I really ought to have called her on arriving home. I have never got into the habit of doing that, even with my children. They used to complain about it but they've got used to me.

I recalled the journey home, cocooned in the heat of the car. Apart from the practised concentration of driving I was detached from my surroundings, oblivious of weather and landscape. I recalled a moment, just as I was approaching Leominster, when I had noticed the weather. The raindrops on the windscreen were thick and shaped like blackberries - sleet. But there had been no trouble with flooding - Linda's understandable fear.

In the evening, I struggled to write the letter that been occupying my mind all day. Thank goodness for word-processing, for being able to re-write as much as you need without getting lost in waste paper.

Dearest Linda,

Even before I start, I know this letter will be a jumble of thoughts and feelings, because I am struggling to do justice to what has happened.

I tried to write a poem about us but gave up. Whenever I went back to it, it looked contrived and so I thought I would just write down the things I am longing to say in the form of a letter, even though I may not send it.

The love we had all those years ago has come back to life. For me, at least. I didn't dare ask you to be explicit about how you felt towards me. I never imagined it to be possible. I didn't know I was still capable of feeling this way - just the same as then. But, can it be the same love? Surely that withered and died 50 years ago.

I loved Margaret completely, and I know you loved John in the same way. We were both true to them for the whole of our marriages, our devotion lasting until they died. So, there should be no connection between our love of now and our love of back then, before our marriages. But they are connected - not by anything alive and active but by something tenuous, invisible, unrecognized until now.

I have an image of a fine golden thread extending through time, or in some other dimension. I also thought of a rhizome, deep in the earth. The plant flourishes and then dies - or seems to. It will not be seen again in the same place. But beneath the ground is its rhizome. This persists, completely hidden and unknown. Then, in another place, a new shoot bursts forth into the light.

Am I assuming too much? We haven't spoken much about our feelings so far - we've only expressed them in other ways. I can only hope you feel as I do.

Having completed it - or rather reached the point where I knew it wasn't going to get any better - I found I'd lost the email address that she'd given me. I decided I would hand-write it and send it as a proper letter.

I went out to post it right away, not wanting to leave it till morning in case I changed my mind 'in the cold light of day'.

13

A bright, dry morning at the start of March, and I had woken up feeling enthusiastic about everything. After breakfast I decided to go for a walk by the river, with the intention of visiting the salt marsh on the way back, especially some parts I hadn't seen since the autumn.

At the side of the footpath, between patches of grass, the ground was wet and dark with dead leaves, throwing into contrast the bright yellows of primroses and celandines. At head-height and above, the bare branches of alders and willows were adorned by catkins.

I left the path and climbed down to the mud flats. My progress was now much slower but I was in no hurry. I enjoyed having to concentrate, to negotiate the network of muddy creeks, their different depths and widths, their strange geometry. Some were clearly visible, others hidden, signalled only by grey-green fringes of sea-purslane. Some could be jumped across, others had to be skirted round. Eventually I came to the bend in the river and decided to take a short cut across the higher, drier ground, through tall reeds.

As I emerged from the reeds I came across a party of students from the nearby field-centre. They were engaged in time-honoured practical ecology activities - working along a line transect that stretched from the highest ground down to the main channel, putting down wire-frame quadrats, and identifying the plants in the sample areas so enclosed.

I spent some time talking with them, resisting the temptation to help when they seemed to be struggling with identification. I then had a longer conversation with their tutors - a man I knew from the staff of the field centre and a woman from the visiting students' own college. Finally, I took some photographs of seasonal interest and headed for home with the intention of telephoning Linda, or perhaps writing to her.

Linda and I had settled quickly into a pattern. One of us would phone the other in the morning and again at night. Sometimes we would write letters - proper letters: hand-written or, if done on the computer, sent as hard copy. Which is odd, come to think of it, because I like to do what is rational - and that would be to use email. But we seldom do - and then only to send attachments. Our letters often crossed in the post and, of course, didn't arrive until one or more days later. Even so, it just felt more comfortable - and familiar.

On arriving home I found that she had phoned me, and had left a short message. I called her and, while waiting for her to answer, I glanced at the calendar. Exactly a fortnight to go before I'll be seeing her. She will be driving down to visit her daughter in Exeter. Then she is going to break the return journey to stay with me for a couple of days before going home.

"Miss Thomas? Will you take a call from a 261 Craftsman Rowe in Bielefeld?"

"Oh yes. I remember him. Twp as ever."

After that silly beginning our conversation flagged and all I could come up with to fill the silence was something I had been thinking about the previous evening: something I intended to ask her about her work on Eric's book. Until then, whenever I raised the subject, she had been reluctant to talk about it, protesting that I wouldn't be at all interested. But my curiosity had been growing and I wanted to try again.

Failing once more to get a response I thought of something that might persuade her: "I did tell you, didn't I, that a few years after getting my chemistry degree, I went on to get an M.Sc.?"

"Yes?"

"I thought I had. But I don't think I ever said what the subject was."

"No, I don't think you did."

"Well, I couldn't use the work I was doing in my job. That was applied research, commercial and not really suitable and my employers wouldn't have approved, so I chose something I could do by private study: the history and philosophy of science."

She said nothing, so I began to talk about my interest in the history of science. I had been holding forth for a few minutes when I felt there was something about her silence, something I was missing.

"Is anything wrong?" I asked. "You've gone very quiet."

"No, nothing's wrong. It's just that I feel a bit overwhelmed. You've got a bee in your bonnet about something."

"I'm sorry!"

"I should think so! I was looking forward to a different sort of talk. Do you know what day this is?"

"Well, it's not your birthday - that's October. So, what day is it?"

"It's the fifth of March - the fifth of March, 2007. Think about that."

Helped by a few clues, I eventually remembered: "Of course - the day we met! This is the fiftieth anniversary of the day we met - in that restaurant."

"Yes! So, let's talk about other things."

"All right," I said. "I'll leave my bee-in-the-bonnet for later."

"Good idea!"

"How did you come to know the exact date? Was it something you remembered?"

"I was going to tell you about that. I used to keep diaries in my younger days; and I wondered if I might still have some of them in the loft. Well, there they were - including the 1957 one. It's full of gaps, mind you, especially after we started going out, but our meeting was fully documented!"

"That's amazing! Bring it with you. Do you mind me reading it?"

"I certainly do."

"Oh. . . that's a pity. What else is in it?"

"A bit about our first date at the pictures. And a bit later there's a mention of you performing in the college skiffle-group. I'd forgotten all about that but it suddenly came to me - a picture in my head of you playing one of those double-bass things made from a tea chest and a broom handle. I seem to remember you played the guitar as well, didn't you?"

"Yes, that's right."

"And didn't you have an electric guitar - one that you'd made yourself?"

"Well, sort of - not really. Skiffle groups didn't use electric guitars. And proper electric guitars weren't around much in Britain until a year or so later. I didn't actually make it - all I did was amplify my acoustic guitar by attaching a throat mike to it."

"Attaching a what?"

"A throat microphone - as used by pilots. You could buy them in military surplus shops."

"I remember some of the tunes," she said. "Quirky American folk songs."

"Yes, that's right."

"Unlike you," she went on, "I've never had any musical ability. That was something I didn't inherit with my Welshness."

"I'm not musical!" I protested. "I was just a three-chord-wonder. I had the ability to play by ear - I could accompany simple songs, that's all."

"Is that as far as it went?"

"Well, I did go a bit further. I took some piano lessons later on but I never played in public any more. I've just remembered: I actually wrote a couple of songs - ballads. That was around 1963. Bacharach and David were my first inspiration - and then The Beatles."

At that point I heard my door-bell ringing. It was someone delivering a parcel. After I had dealt with it, Linda said that she "ought to be getting on" and so we brought things to a close. I said I would write to her later in the day.

§

14

<u>*The Fifth of March, Two Thousand and Seven - TA DA!*</u>

Dearest Linda,
Since talking to you this morning I've been thinking about this being our 50th anniversary. Not being able to do anything on the day itself, I thought we could do something special in the way of celebration when you're here in two weeks time. I have an idea - how would you like a couple of days in Cornwall? My favourite part is Mount's Bay - right down the westernmost end. It's beautiful there - the whole bay has got something special about it - and I know some good places where we could stay. Being early in the year, and before Easter, there should be plenty of accommodation available. Let me know what you think.

To continue with what I wanted to say to you - that 'bee in my bonnet'. Science has been my thing ever since childhood, and from primary school days it was a big part of my reading (along with the Wizard, the Rover and the Eagle) The books that I particularly enjoyed were those that told the story of discovery or showed the history of the way ideas developed. Later, at school and college, it suited me that many of the concepts in chemistry and physics were taught in this historical way. For my M.Sc. dissertation I chose a topic within the history of ideas concerning atoms and molecules.

Sorry if I seem to be going on about this, but I'm still hoping to persuade you to tell me more about the work you were doing with Eric. Back in the 50s I was also quite interested in psychology. Do you remember? - I used to go on about Freud and psychoanalysis. And now I'd better change the subject.

How is your friend Dawn. I expect she's out of hospital by now. Come to think of it, you can tell me about her when I phone to wish you goodnight - which will be before this reaches you!

With love,
Mike

<u>6th March 2007</u>

Dearest Mike,
Thank you for your letter which has just arrived. I hope you won't mind if I say 'No - not this time' to your suggestion of a trip to Cornwall. I'm usually exhausted after staying with Sarah and Dan and their boisterous children and I won't feel like travelling about much. I shall be looking forward to a nice rest, in Devon. It will be treat enough to be looked after and waited on by you.

As I mentioned on the phone, Dawn is a lot better. In fact, she is now convalescing at home. I'm going round to see her tonight.

<u>The bee in your bonnet</u>
Of course I'm willing to tell you about the work with Eric, but I still don't think it will be of much interest to you.

I may have misled you about the extent of my involvement. For much of the time I was just helping with literature searches, editing, and secretary stuff, although I was able to make a few contributions of my own to the first part. Eric had no experience of the classical philosophers. He had got into psychology from a natural sciences background. I was in a position to point him in the right direction in a few places, having learnt a bit from living and working with John.

Eric's original plan was unexceptional - and realistic. But there were a lot of new things being published in that area, and he was determined to include everything and not be left behind - shades of Casaubon, again! Also, while what he started with was a straightforward, narrative history, much of this new writing was concerned with so-called 'critical' psychology - more modern, even 'post-modern' approaches. The sort of thing he started with - a progressive history of ideas - was likely to be dismissed as 'celebratory' and 'Whiggish' by some of his contemporaries. He went on adding more and more to his original plan, anxious not to miss anything, anxious not to be considered out of date - or naive.

I think he lost his way. At the time I parted company with him, he was talking of re-doing the whole thing as a 'metahistory' as he called it - a history of histories of psychology. I hope he finishes his project - but I have my doubts.

There, that will do for now! I'll bring my copy of the first volume - the part that actually got published. It might satisfy you - or at least stop you going on about it.

I hope you won't think I'm being 'reproachful' (again) but I found your letter a disappointment after the nice romantic ones you've been sending me.

I send you my love (even though you sometimes don't deserve it).

Linda

§

15

Linda pointed down to the iron ring set into the stonework.

"Is that where you used to tie up your boat?"

"That's right. I'm thinking of getting another - it looks empty down there now."

She had arrived, looking tired, at about 6.00 the previous evening. After going out for a celebratory meal, with champagne, we had returned to the house to sit and listen to music before having an early night. She seemed much brighter next morning; and we spent a couple of hours just gossiping, ending up standing by the sea wall at the bottom of the garden.

I added, "And that's my own little bit of salt marsh over there. I've watched it develop. When we first moved here it was just a patch of rocks and mud, submerged at high tide. When the water was clear I could watch crabs emerging from under the rocks and moving about. But, gradually, the silt accumulated and it turned into that little mud bank. First it was colonised by different kinds of algae, and then marsh samphire, followed by. . ." I thought I saw a trace of that polite look I get when I'm enthusing about things. I quickly finished: "Ecological successions always fascinate me - even on a small scale."

She gave me a smile before hunching her shoulders. "I'm beginning to feel cold - do you mind if we go back inside?"

In the kitchen once more, I put together a lunch of vegetable soup, cheese and rolls while Linda disappeared upstairs. When she came down she was carrying a large envelope. "Here it is," she said: "Volume One. Having gone to the trouble of bringing it I want to make sure I give it to you."

"Thanks. I'll look at it after lunch."

As soon as we had finished eating, I went up to fetch my M.Sc. dissertation. I put it down in front of her on the kitchen table.

"So," she said, "it's 'I'll show you mine if you'll show me yours' is it?" She opened the envelope and took out a thick book in a plain grey dust jacket. I handed her my slim, quarto-sized effort in its black binding.

I started by reading the introduction and then began to skim and glance through the first few chapters. Eventually I stopped and looked at Linda, waiting for her to look up before I said, "This first part - about the Greek and Roman philosophers - I didn't think psychology went back that far. When would you say it began?"

"Well," she replied, "there's no simple answer to that. It depends what you mean by psychology, doesn't it?"

"I suppose so."

"Someone once wrote that 'psychology has a long past but only a short history'."

"Who wrote that?"

"A 19th century gentleman with a big beard - Hermann Ebbinghaus. He's famous for being a pioneer researcher on memory."

"So, when was the 'psychology' word first used?"

"In its present day sense, not before the 18th Century."

I thought of something that seemed relevant, if a bit obvious: "I suppose psychology really started with philosophy, didn't it?"

She nodded. "That certainly applies to academic psychology."

"And, as you told me, that's where your expertise was useful to Eric."

"I'm not an expert! I picked up a lot from living with John, helping with his teaching materials, and things for publication. I've read quite a bit too, but I'm only self-taught. I haven't got any qualifications, have I?" She then looked at me, rather quizzically "You seem bothered."

"I was just thinking. . . I find it. . . amazing, bewildering. . ."

"What do you find amazing and bewildering?"

"That you've become so academic."

She laughed. "You're flummoxed! Your little girl-friend from 1957 has turned into an egg-head!"

"Don't mock me! I need time to grasp it all. The different lives we've led. All those years - all the different things we've been doing. I'm still trying to match up the way we were then and the way we are now."

"I know," she said, reaching to pat my forearm. "We're so different now. But we still feel connected - it's your rhizome, isn't it?"

I couldn't think of anything else to add that wouldn't spoil the moment, so I stood up. "Tea or coffee?"

"Tea please."

When I sat down again I noticed she was well into my dissertation. "What do you make of it?" I asked.

"I can follow some of it - not the mathematical bits, though. Tell me the gist - give me a summary."

"Well, I'm a bit rusty - it's a long time since I was concerned with physical chemistry. It's about a controversy from the 19th century. More Victorian gents with beards! - although maybe I shouldn't say 'Victorian' because most of them were continentals. People had come up with idea of molecules - the smallest particles of a substance. It was a useful hypothesis - physicists could use it to explain the properties of gases and liquids. And chemists used it to account for. . . well, all sorts of things, to do with chemical combination. But no-one had ever *seen* molecules - they would have to be so small as to make that impossible at the time." I stopped.

"Go on," she said. "The idea of atoms goes back to the Greeks and I know about molecules from trying to take an interest in Heulwen's homework, when she was doing her A Levels."

16

I suggested we drive to Hartland - a spectacular bit of coast whatever the weather and tide, and one of my favourite nearby places.

Soon after we set out she remarked: "You were going to tell me more about Margaret."

"Oh, yes," I replied, but then didn't know where to begin.

"You said you met in Bedford when you were living in the same house." "That's right. We had adjacent bed-sits and we shared a kitchen and bathroom."

"Tell me again - what were you doing there?"

"My first proper job after leaving the army. I was a laboratory assistant, doing applied research in organic chemistry. Margaret worked for the same firm, different department. She was a lab assistant as well, but working with plants." I paused.

"Go on."

"That was when my life seemed to start again. That brand new feeling, like the song. After leaving the army I'd had no real sense of where I was going. Back home in Essex, living with Mum and Dad, I went from job to job for about two years before I found this one. As soon as I started there, I learned that my employers gave day-release for study. Some of the other assistants, including Maggie, were going to the nearby college, day and evenings, to study externally for London University degrees. The timing was just right: it was November when I started and Maggie - we'd only just met - pointed out there was still time to register for that academic

"Whose homework?"

"Hayley. Heulwen is her real name but she decided to call herself Hayley when she was about thirteen."

"Oh. . . " I cut some pieces from the sponge cake I had brought in with the tea. "Well, as time went on, some chemists began to get the idea of molecules having an actual, three-dimensional shape - the atoms they were made of sticking out and having definite positions in space. But other people were dead against treating molecules as if they had this literal, physical existence. Regarding them as little objects seemed wrong. . ."

"Reification!" said Linda.

"What?"

"A kind of error - you sometimes come across it when people are theorising or speculating. It means treating abstract concepts as if they are 'things' - actual objects. Could it be that that's what they were wary of doing?"

"Yes, it might have been that. Come to think of it, not long before that time, some chemists were thinking that heat was an actual substance - they called it 'caloric'. Then the idea of energy came along, and. . . Yes, I suppose it was that sort of thing."

She closed the book and looked at me. "Who would have thought, back then, that we'd be having this sort of conversation? You're all dumbfounded about the way *I've* changed - well, what about *you*? You've changed. Your letter - the golden thread one - you were always a bit of a romantic, but now you're quite a poet. And a botanist - you never used to show any interest in plants."

"Ah, that was Margaret's influence. I'll tell you about her later. Let's go out for a drive while the weather looks OK."

§

I took her hand and squeezed it. "Thank you for correcting my ignorance! But, *Shirley* that's got nothing to do with it. *Shirley* you don't believe that forgetory is as meaningful as memory, do you?"

"I didn't say I did. It just occurred to me that we use the word memory in too simple, too concrete a sense. It's that reification again! Is memory a *thing*, any more than forgetory?"

"Well, it may not be a 'thing' but. . ." I stopped myself saying 'Shirley' again, ". . .remembering is still the positive process whereas forgetting isn't - it's just a failure - something negative."

"Freud didn't think so, did he?"

"Oh well, if you're going to bring *him* into it. I wasn't thinking of repression."

"And it's long been thought that being able to forget may be necessary for our sanity."

I had nothing to say in reply to that and things went quiet. Then I commented on how impressed I was at her knowledge.

She shrugged. "Memory was one of the big themes Eric was exploring. We talked about it a lot."

§

17

It was during the evening, in the dining room, at the end of our meal, that I reminded Linda she had been promising to tell me more about her early life with John. "You told me it was October 1959," I prompted, "but how did you actually meet?"

"It was at a church function."

"Which church was that?"

"The Anglican - the one I used to go to with Mum. She was church, wasn't she, Dad was chapel."

"So, what happened?"

"He asked me out."

I waited for more, then I asked: "Can you remember when it was, exactly, that we split up? I know it was towards the end of the summer."

"According to my diary, I sent you the last letter - the 'Dear John' as you called it - on September the 24th."

"So you sent me a 'Dear John' just before getting off with a John! You didn't wait long, did you?"

"Well, there was something about him that felt right. You told me you felt like that when you first got to know Margaret." She told me more about what had attracted her to him. My earlier impressions were being confirmed: she saw him as a man of character, with strengths and important attributes. After a while I began to say something along those lines.

"But he wasn't perfect!" she protested, and then, obviously anxious to reassure, she spoke about some of their differences.

It worked - I began to feel better, realising how over-sensitive I had been. Still at the back of my mind was that old, embedded attitude towards myself as the feckless failure, the big let-down.

Eventually her concern for my feelings began to be too much for me. To change the subject, I asked: "Where did you live after you got married?"

"We had a flat." She gave its location, but was strangely vague about it.

Suddenly I cottoned on and gleefully asked: "Do you mean a certain terrace of tall Victorian houses, facing the sea?"

"That's right - a few doors from where I'd been living on my own - my 'room with a view'."

That really did change the subject. We returned to the fraught time when, after relations with her parents - mainly her father - had deteriorated so badly, she had run away from home to live in a little attic room. This crisis had occurred at a bad time - she'd had to cope on her own because my unit was just about to be posted to Germany.

Recalling these events I was suddenly overwhelmed by a resurgence of feelings. Guilt, anxiety for her welfare - made worse by the knowledge that we would soon be separated by insurmountable distance.

I could picture that room in minute detail. I had stayed there on only two occasions - the first in the autumn, on leave, before my unit embarked; and the second in the early summer, during the one UK leave granted me from my exile. It should have been the second that I remembered - the joy of being with Linda in the summer; the vistas from her window of bright blue sea, the headlands, and in the distance the hills of the Lleyn Peninsula, looking like islands. But my mood determined that I should recall the first time - the darkness, the dreary weather, the constant, intrusive howling of the wind.

I was re-living this time, describing it to her at length, when she stopped me with an angry outburst: "You were only there for two days! Then you were able to go and stay with your mum and dad before sailing to Germany! I had to live through the whole of that winter on my own!" All the previous reassurance was undone - I was being utterly selfish; she was the one who had suffered; and it was my fault.

Then something wonderful and restoring happened. Having been sitting on either side of the table, we suddenly got to our feet and stumbled to find each other.

When we spoke again it was of other, present things - mainly to do with her departure the following day. One of the things we talked of was a piece of news she had forgotten until then to pass on to me. It was that Gwen and Dennis had suggested to her that we go and stay with them sometime soon. They had suggested early in May.

§

18

I managed to be up with the light that May morning to make an early start, so I reached Linda's house at about 1.00pm.

After a quick lunch we set out. I assumed we were heading directly for Wales but she insisted that we deliver something to a friend first. This meant traffic problems and going in the opposite direction for a while. The errand didn't seem urgent to me, and could have waited till we came back in four days time. I pointed this out; and that led to an argument and a cold heavy silence for the first half of the journey.

It was late afternoon, warm and bright, when we arrived. Gwen and Dennis, both dressed in shorts and T-shirts, greeted us at the gate and then led the way to a small garden behind the house, enclosed by out-buildings and trees. They urged us not to bother with luggage and things until later and to come and share afternoon tea with them right away.

After a few minutes I felt the need to stand and walk about - I was still stiff from driving all day. I began exploring the garden, a part of their home I'd hardly looked at on my previous visit. I remarked upon the trees - not fully out yet - and spoke about this time of year when the leaves are brand new.

"All those beautiful shades of green," put in Gwen. She turned to Dennis. "Show them your painting."

"Not now," he replied, seeming a bit embarrassed.

"These trees are a bit behind," Gwen continued, "the ones in the lane have been out for days. Sometimes it seems to happen all at once - you go along the lane one day and the trees are still sort of transparent; and then, two days later, they've gone opaque."

Dennis lit a cigarette but had barely begun it when Gwen protested: "Your smoke is going all over Linda! You'll have to smoke somewhere else."

"All right," said Dennis, "I know - I'm a pariah." He stood up. "Come on Mike, let's go for a walk. I've got something to show you - something that should interest you. It wasn't here last time you came."

"You can show him that later," said Gwen. "I don't want you disappearing - it isn't polite, is it. All right, you can stay here and smoke, but sit down-wind of us."

"I don't mind a bit of smoke," said Linda. "I used to smoke myself, once upon a time."

"Neither do I," I added. "We were all smokers back then, weren't we?" That reminded me of something I'd recalled recently. "Do you remember 'firing squad' - that trick we used to get up to in the corner cafe?" They looked puzzled and I continued: "We used to make guns - we'd take the metal foil from cigarette packets and wrap it around the heads of matches. I forget how we propped them up, but we'd aim them, and apply a lighted match to the foil, and out would shoot the match-stick."

"Oh, yes," said Dennis, eventually.

"Yes, I remember you boys getting up to that trick," said Gwen. "I used to think it was dangerous - I'd been brought up not to play with fire. Now, let's talk about something sensible. I want to hear what you two have been getting up to."

Linda looked at me as though she wanted me to begin, so I started giving a short account of our times together. Some bits they would have known about already, but I wasn't sure which. I finished by asking "And what have *you* two been doing?"

Dennis described their winter holiday in Italy - something I knew about in bare outline from the post-card I got in February. My attention wandered and I remember little of what he said. After making some more tea and bringing more food, Gwen told us about visits to theatres and what their choral society had been doing; and she mentioned in passing that Dennis had recently taken up water-colour painting.

Following a pause, Gwen looked up and then got to her feet. "It's getting chilly out here now that we've lost the sun - shall we go inside?"

"Let me take some photos first," I said. After I'd done so I went to get our things from the car.

When I rejoined them, in the kitchen, I was struck by the change in mood - they were in the middle of a subdued conversation about the recent deaths of two of Linda's and Gwen's school-friends. This led to reflections about this time in later life when you get news of the illnesses and deaths of friends and acquaintances with increasing frequency. I recalled my mother once complaining that everyone she knew seemed to be dying or dead.

This led to mention of another college friend called Kate, not known to me. Gwen described her, and explained that she had studied 'agri bot' - agricultural botany - for her degree. She then added "After she graduated she went to work in Hertfordshire, at Rothamsted Experimental Station. That's in your old neck of the woods isn't it?"

"I know Rothamsted" I said. "That's where Maggie used to work, before we met."

"We went to stay with her once while she was there," put in Dennis. "She showed us round the place."

A few minutes later the sun suddenly returned and shone through the kitchen window. "Let's go for a walk," said Dennis.

"There's only time for a short one," warned Gwen. "I've got cooking to do."

We set out from a little gate among the trees at the end of the enclosed garden. The sun was behind us, lighting up the hill we were to climb. The path, steep and stony, soon began to narrow, obliging us to walk in single file. As we reached the top of the slope it widened a little and we ended up walking in pairs, Gwen and I leading.

I was telling her more about Margaret, explaining how she had worked at Rothamsted before moving to Bedford where we met. "Maggie took me to Rothamsted once," I said; and an interesting possibility occurred to me: "When Kate showed you round, did she by any chance show you a field - well, a piece of woodland now - that had been left from the previous century, to revert to nature?"

"Yes, she did. There were two, weren't there. I even remember their names - one was called Broadbalk, the other Geescroft."

I was taken aback - to have been met with such specific information just as I was about to explain my own arcane interest. Gwen laughed at my reaction and proceeded to remind me of things I had forgotten: that her first degree had been in geography; and that British soils and vegetation had been what she had researched for her master's degree.

Dennis chose that moment to squeeze between us. "What's this about?"

We stopped walking, waited briefly while Linda caught up, and then Gwen reiterated what had just passed, and went on to explain: "There were these two fields - they'd been used for growing wheat. Then, in the 1880s, they were left, untouched, to see what they'd become." She glanced at me as if to say 'you carry on'.

"And now they've reverted to woodland," I said. "Different trees. . ."

"Oak and ash, hawthorn and holly - that's what I remember," said Gwen. "It was thought that the plots might one day go back to being like ancient, post-glacial woodland. But I wonder now - with global warming - what they'll become."

"This sounds like another of your ecological successions," said Linda.

"Why *your* ecological successions?" asked Dennis, looking at me, puzzled.

"I have an obsession with succession," I replied, trying with a little humour to shrug off my feeling of exposed nerdiness.

Dennis rescued me: "I once shared your fascination," he said. "As a kid I was always setting up miniature ponds. You know - in jam-jars, sweet-jars, buckets. Sometimes I'd start them off with just rain water and see what developed. Soon there would be things you could find with a microscope, like algae, protozoa and rotifers. The jars were seeded by spores in the dust, of course - and that provided nutrients as well - the beginnings of a detritus-based food chain. . ."

Gwen put her arm round Dennis's waist. "We now know the beginnings of *his* succession," she said. "The evolution of a fresh-water biologist - starting with his little jars and progressing to lakes, and rivers."

"And he even migrated to salt water," said Dennis. He put his arm round her and kissed her.

She turned to Linda and me. "Did you like to play around with water when you were little?" We both said yes. "My parents," continued Gwen, "discouraged me from playing with anything that would make me wet - or dirty." She didn't sound at all bitter but it struck me what a deprived childhood she must have had.

"Mine didn't approve," added Linda, then: "Maybe that's why you chose soil as your research subject."

"That's very psychological of you," said Dennis.

"Talking of psychology," said Gwen, "have you seen anything of Eric recently?"

Dennis chose that moment to begin talking to me about his aquatic pursuits and, for the rest of the walk, I wasn't able to hear what passed between the two women.

The route was a circular one and we were soon within sight of the house again. As we entered the garden my attention was caught by something curious: light, of an unusual blue or slightly purple colour, coming from a small window in one of the stone outbuildings.

19

The next morning started grey and wet. After breakfast in the kitchen we lingered over coffee, discussing what we could do that day.

In the evening we were due to go to a party. Only a small affair, Gwen had reassured us, when giving us the news the night before. At least one old acquaintance from college days would be there, she said, as well as someone Linda and Gwen had known from school. Nothing had been decided concerning the rest of the day.

After some time of few suggestions and much speculation about the weather, Dennis looked across the table at me. "I'm going for a smoke. You coming?"

As soon as we got outside he lit up; and then he began walking towards one of the outbuildings. It was the small stone one from which the mysterious light had been shining the day before. "Here's what I wanted to show you yesterday," he said, opening the door.

In the centre was a huge glass aquarium, shallow but broad. Suspended from the beams above were lighting pendants that hung close to the surface of the water. It was a marine aquarium; and more than that, as he explained with much enthusiasm, it was a coral reef set-up. I only knew a little about coral reef ecosystems - mainly from TV nature films - but I recognised some of the organisms. There were different corals, both 'soft' and stony kinds, each with its distinctive polyps. Their little sea-anemone forms were all moving, the tiny tentacles quivering and undulating - not autonomously, he explained to my disappointment, but mainly through the current created by a pump. The colours ranged from reds to browns and purples. Between the corals were forms that I recognised as sea cucumbers and, most colourful of all to my amazement, there were clams, with partly open, wavy lips. Some of these were a fluorescent, almost luminous green, set off by contrasting hues, reminiscent of the green and purple of shot silk but much brighter.

I woke up to the fact that Dennis was going on about the importance of the lights. Something I knew already - that the corals' main source of nutrition was the symbiotic algae living inside their cells. Different lamps, he explained, were there for different purposes - halide lamps and white and blue fluorescent tubes, controlled by timers, were there to simulate morning, day and evening, not to mention giving some ultra-violet to enhance the colours. "Here, have a look at the different spectra," he said, handing me a small spectroscope.

I looked through it and saw the brilliant bands, mainly in the blue and yellow of the spectrum. I handed it back, and commented on something I had noticed earlier. "I didn't see any fishes - are there any?"

"Not at present - just invertebrates. By the way, I approve of your saying 'fishes' for the plural and not 'fish'."

"Schoolteacher!" I taunted. Then I spotted some complicated-looking machinery in the dark space beneath the bench holding the tank. "Is that where the pump is?"

"Yes, and the filters, and the temperature controls, and the skimmer, and other things. I suppose you think it's not very green of me - all the power this consumes." That hadn't occurred to me until he said it.

"This is all very surprising," I replied. "I thought you'd lost interest in biological things."

"Not all. I've just moved on from those aspects that used to excite me most - like physiology and genetics. I still like the forms of animals and plants - the subjects of my paintings."

The door opened behind us and there was Gwen, framed by daylight. "I knew I'd find you in here! Linda and I have decided where we'd like to go."

"And that is. . .?" asked Dennis.

"Bodnant Garden," said Gwen. Linda has never been there."

"I'm hoping to see the famous laburnum tunnel," said Linda.

"Isn't it a bit early for that?" said Dennis. "The laburnums might not be fully in flower."

"We've already had that conversation," replied Gwen. "We ought to leave right away. I think the weather is going to get better."

In spite of the outing being a great success, I find that I remember little about it. When we set out the sky was dark grey although as soon as we found the A5 and began travelling west, the sun came out. For the rest of the journey I put my map away and made the most of the luxury of being driven, able to hill-gaze all along the Conwy Valley.

Linda said how much she enjoyed seeing the tunnel which did look quite impressive, not at all a disappointment. She also said that the garden was gorgeous and that the whole trip was very satisfying and refreshing. I was pleased to hear this because it brought home to me another way in which I had changed since I lost Maggie. We used to visit gardens all over the country and we shared an enthusiasm for gardening ourselves but, since living on my own, the enjoyment had withered - even though my love of wild plants in natural habitats had grown. I hoped that my lack of enthusiasm had not been noticed by the others. Appropriately, all three were fully paid-up members of The National Trust while I had dropped out several years before.

There were some things for which I could share their enthusiasm without pretending: the lake, certain plants in the prime of their flowering, and, not least, the scents.

20

The Morgans lived a few miles away, close to the border, in a large barn-conversion. On arriving we handed over the wine we had bought on the way home from Bodnant and were given glasses of fruity summer punch which we drank while standing on a sun-lit patio, looking around at the other guests. These ranged in age from Cerys and Tom Morgan's children, in their 20s and 30s, to men and women of similar seniority to the four of us.

The punch was pleasant - and rather strong, consisting largely, I found out, of home made white wine. By my third glass, on an empty stomach, I had become rather garrulous and was soon engaged in lively conversations with various people including an old college acquaintance called Bob - the one Dennis had mentioned. We had done chemistry together. I remembered him chatting up the pretty girl who used to bring tea and doughnuts round to us at our laboratory benches. We reflected on the horrified reaction such service would evoke in these health and safety times.

Some time later, after we had all gone inside to eat, I was standing close to Linda and Gwen. They were talking with Cerys and Tom and they seemed to be enjoying a gossip that didn't involve me. I didn't mind; in my present state I was happy just to be there, on the edge.

There came a point, after they had been laughing uproariously at something, when their language morphed from English to Welsh. Unlike some non-Welsh speaking people I have never minded this but I felt a touch of vicarious embarrassment as I looked around in case any others within earshot had noticed and not approved. A woman of auburn hair and indeterminate age was standing nearby. She signalled her concern by raising her eyes. Then she came across and stood by me.

"Do you speak Welsh?" I asked.

She shook her head. "Not well enough. I learnt it at school, and my vocabulary is quite good, but my family only spoke English at home."

By enquiring where school and home were, I quickly realised that she was Jenny, the school friend.

"How long have you known Linda?" she asked.

"About four months."

She looked at me curiously. "Gwen said you and Linda were old friends from way back."

"Well, yes - I had known her previously, a very long time ago."

"When was that?"

"Back in the 1950s. I was a student and she was working at the town hall." Jenny continued to look at me in the same way. I added, "Dennis and I were students together. We were from the same school. You were at school with Linda and Gwen, weren't you?"

"Yes," she replied, her expression changing to one of puzzled interest. "Did you know John, her husband."

"No, I never met him. I knew her before he came along." Her expression didn't change. "What was he like?" I asked, hoping to shift her unsettling attention from me, but also out of curiosity.

"Nice man. Rather quiet, very intelligent." She said a few more things but I learned little from them.

I had been noticing her pale and freckled face. She had probably been a natural redhead and her hair, now obviously dyed, looked quite authentic. I wondered how old she was. "Were you in the same year as Gwen?"

She smiled. "Do you mind - I'm two years younger than that! I was in Linda's class." Her intent expression suddenly returned. "You would have known her previous boy-friend - the one before she started going out with John."

I gave no response. It had occurred to me, as soon as I learnt who she was, that she might recognise me, even though I didn't remember her. But I was caught on the hop by this question and I froze. "Would you like another drink," I asked, eventually.

The moment I got back and handed her the glass she said "Thanks. You must have known him - he was a student, about the same time as you - although he didn't last long." I sipped my drink and said nothing. "I never actually met him," she went on, "but I used to see him around and hear things about him. He was an excitable sort of person. Rather manic, I got the impression - a bit loopy. He failed his exams and had to leave. Then he got called up for National Service. Linda stuck by him for a long time but it was too much for her in the end. She fell out with her parents because of him and left home." She looked hard at me. "And you don't remember him?" Then her look changed once more. "Oh shit... It's you, isn't it?"

I forget my reply, if any. I just remember emptying my glass while she tried to get over her embarrassment.

At that point we were interrupted by music. While we had been talking, some of the guests - a mixture of old and young - had gathered at one end of the room and now began singing to acoustic guitars and mandolin. Others began to move about and find seats.

Dennis appeared from somewhere and then he, Linda and Gwen came over to Jenny and me and the five of us ended up sitting round a little table near the musicians. Folk songs - one in Welsh, the rest in English - were the order of the day; and the audience joined in the singing. This was the stuff I enjoyed at my local folk club in Devon: guitars, melodeon, tin whistle - no electronics, no amplifiers. I closed my eyes to listen.

I woke with an awareness of alarm - not so much a feeling as a notion in my present state. I had drunk too much. Linda was our driver this evening, and I had taken too much advantage of her gallant offer to abstain. The music had stopped, our impromptu folk group having dispersed, although someone was producing odd notes and chords on a guitar.

Gwen and Linda were talking about the college jazz band of those days and old acquaintances among its members.

Jenny turned to me and said quietly "They called themselves 'Cambrensis', didn't they?" I nodded. "Didn't you perform with them. . . while you were there?"

"No. I was never a good enough musician. But a couple of them used to play in the skiffle group with me. You might be thinking of that." This was the last thing I said to her because I managed to avoid her for the rest of the evening.

§

20

We left the Morgans' about 11.30, Linda driving carefully under a starless sky. We were in a musical mood and sang various favourite songs including some from our college days. The mood persisted after we arrived home. I would have preferred to go to bed but the others wanted to stay up and talk and drink coffee and I went along with them. I was sobering up, that was the problem, and just beginning to get a hint of hangover - a sense of melancholic emptiness that I don't usually feel until the next morning.

For ten minutes or so, I talked with Linda and Dennis while Gwen played the piano. She suddenly got up and left the room; and then re-appeared carrying a guitar. "Here, Mike - your turn to give us a song."

"Not me - it's been far too long!"

She ignored my protest. "You'll have to tune it - it's been in a cupboard for years."

I took it. "OK. Give me an E." She struck the note on the piano and I began. Some of the strings were very slack, and I took my time, trying to think of what to play. "What about you Dennis?" I tried to hand it to him.

"Not me - I can't play any instruments - except the kazoo, or paper and comb. You're stuck with it Mike. Come on – we're waiting."

I tried out a few chords before I began to play, and sing 'Unchained Melody'.

When I finished, they clapped, and Gwen said "Well done, Mike. Let's have some more golden oldies."

My next was 'Trains and boats and planes' followed by 'Sealed with a kiss'.

Gwen protested: "Can we have something more cheerful - not just loss and separation?"

"Give us one of your own compositions," suggested Linda. My hesitation prompted her to remind me: "You told me you had written some ballads. You said you had once been inspired by Bacharach and The Beatles."

"No, that's enough - I've done my duty. Anyway, they're not good enough for public performance." I said nothing of my other reason: Gwen's remark had made me realise that my own pieces were just as sentimental, if not more so.

At that moment a large moth collided with the lampshade. Dennis managed to catch it and went over to the window to release it. "There are lots of moths out here - it reminds me of the summer term in. . . 1957. We were in the parlour at *Ty Glas* - supposed to be swotting for the exams. Do you remember? It was very hot, so we opened the window but had to close it again because we kept being bombarded by cockchafers and moths."

"It's quite warm tonight," said Gwen. "I'd like to sit outside. I don't mind the moths." No-one responded to her suggestion.

"I don't recall that," I said, replying to Dennis. "I might not have been there."

"I'm not surprised," he responded. "You didn't stay in much around that time. You were probably out with Linda. You weren't one to do much swotting, were you - until the exams. And then. . ." He went quiet.

Something reminded me of the photos I had taken that day, and I went to get my camera to have a look at them and show them to the others. They didn't seem interested. I then made the mistake of going on about memories and photos. Linda tactfully shut me up by referring to our previous conversation about memory and ageing.

"We've got nothing to complain about," said Dennis. "When I think of some of my relations and acquaintances."

"Please," said Gwen, "if we're going to talk, let's go outside."

After we had settled ourselves on the patio, with some snacks that Gwen had got together, Dennis went on: "I'd been thinking about how fortunate the four of us are, considering our age. We all seem to be in good health. None of us has had hip-replacement. We're all *compos mentis*. No-one seems to be unduly deaf. I might be putting my foot in it, of course - Mike and Linda may suffer from decrepitudes that we don't know about."

Linda said, "Friends of mine, some younger then me, have had cancer, and other serious illnesses." She turned to Gwen. "Same for you, I expect."

Gwen nodded, and was quiet for a few seconds. Then she said, "It's my failing sight that bothers me. I'm all right in the daytime, and for reading, thank goodness - but I don't drive any more; and that's something I miss." Then her tone changed to one of scornful amusement. "Old Mr Hypochondria here likes to worry over everything and nothing." Dennis grunted. "At the moment it's his colour vision. And last year he thought he was losing his sense of smell."

"That would be a great loss to me," I said, surprised at how alarmed I felt at just the mention of the possibility.

I must have gone into some sort of reverie at that point and, when I came to, the others were talking about the party. It was Gwen mentioning the name 'Jenny' that had caught my attention. She was asking Linda what it had been like to meet her old friend after all those years and to hear how her life had progressed.

"She wasn't exactly a close friend," said Linda. She turned to me. "You were talking to Jenny for quite a while. Did you recognise her?"

"No - we never actually met back then. But she knew about me and she. . . soon realised who I was."

22

We agreed to start the return journey to Shrewsbury at about midday. Just before leaving, I managed to persuade Dennis to show us a couple of his paintings. He was reluctant at first and kept saying, "next time"; but he gave in eventually and took us into his studio/workroom. On display were several watercolours but my attention was caught by two large acrylics. One was a pale blue under-seascape full of bizarre organic forms, mostly translucent and in many subdued colours. The second was a forest scene, rather Rousseauesque and almost entirely in greens. He then told us about a forthcoming project - his 'muriel' as he referred to it. A bare white wall at the back of the house was going to be graced with a huge naturalistic painting. He had been planning it for some time. "You can see it on your next visit," he said, "unless it's been painted over white again." This led to talk of the future and vague plans of getting together later in the summer. Then, after affectionate farewells all round, we set out.

At some point while I was driving, Linda began talking about the party and asked: "Are you sure you never met Jenny back in the old days?"

"I'm positive."

"She seemed to remember you - although I suppose that could be by reputation."

"Well, she didn't recognise me. It was only at the end of our conversation that the penny dropped and she realised I was your earlier boyfriend - the disreputable one. So, what did she say about me?"

"Not much," she replied. "It was only just before we were leaving that she mentioned things."

"Such as what?"

"Well, she reminded me of the time when you and the other students were taking those purple heart pills - to help you swot for the exams, that's what you told me. It was amphetamine, wasn't it? And you weren't just taking them when studying, were you. I'd forgotten until she mentioned it but you were sometimes a bit. . . well, 'strange' when you were out and about with me, weren't you?"

Alarm and shame - a time I hadn't wanted us jointly to remember. I told her how I felt and even added a bit of confession:

"It was more than just purple hearts. We got those from the doctor on prescription and a lot of the students were using them, as you know. But I was also messing with some yellow pills that one of the chemistry students had got hold of. They also contained amphetamine. You know how much I still regret that time."

She remained silent. I construed this as more memory and disapproval of my lack of character in those days. But when she spoke again it turned out that it was my behaviour at the party that was bothering her.

"You had too much to drink, and you were very chatty," she said eventually. I began to defend myself, saying that I didn't realise how strong the punch was until, being very thirsty that day, I'd guzzled too much of it.

"But you carried on drinking, didn't you? I'm worried that you're a bit too fond of alcohol. When I said I'd do the driving you jumped on my offer with unseemly haste."

The journey continued in near silence. I tried to think of something I could say or do that would raise the mood but nothing came to mind and, for a while, all I could do was brood on my resolve to go without booze that evening, to show her. Bleak and dreary were my thoughts and feelings -

reminding me again of the past - and, as then, I felt shut out and incapable.

By the time we were approaching Linda's house things had improved. I can't recall what had got us talking again - I think it was something very ordinary and practical. The nearest thing to a sharp exchange happened when I mentioned the party again and referred to Jenny as her old friend.

"She was never really a friend!" said Linda. "She could be spiteful at times - and a trouble-maker. She was also a fantasist - very good at making things up and coming to believe them. Have you ever known someone like that?" I couldn't think of anyone.

Just before arriving we dropped in at a super-market to buy a Thai meal for two to take home. When I ostentatiously declared that I wouldn't be buying any wine, Linda retorted, "Well I'm having some."

Later, while waiting in the dining room for Linda to heat and serve the food, I began to look around at the photos of John and of Heulwen and Sarah on their graduation days. This gave me an idea and later, during the meal, I said how much I would like to see some photographs of their life when the children were young and before John died.

As soon as we had finished, Linda went to search for them while I washed up. She returned carrying several albums and said, "There you are. You will let me know when you've seen enough - please don't be polite."

It was Linda looking bored that finally made me stop. I had been finding it fascinating, compelling, to follow the pictorial narrative of all that life, all that time, hitherto unknown to me. There she was, with hair not quite beehive but definitely 1960s, and a miniskirt. Later, long flowing hair and skirt, with flowers and beads. At some point John had grown a beard and maintained it until the 1980s. Their girls seemed to change in fits and starts as growth spurts and changing fashions rendered them briefly unrecognisable. The settings were the stages and ceremonial rites of life - birthdays and

Christmases, holidays and outings, school uniforms, sports events, concerts.

I began, inevitably, to express my regret about not having albums full of photos and other such aids to memory. Linda stopped me: "For goodness' sake, stop fretting about forgetting!"

§

23

Linda was up some time before me. As soon as I had showered and dressed I went to look for her. After glancing in the kitchen, dining room, study and bedroom, I returned to the kitchen, puzzled, and made myself a cup of tea. Eventually she emerged through the back door from the garden.

"I wondered where you'd got to," I said.

"I've been enjoying the flowers, and the bird-song."

I noticed then that she was drenched with rainwater. "How long have you been out there?"

She gave me a teasing look, in anticipation of my surprise. "I got up at five. I've been for a long walk. It wasn't raining then!"

"Why didn't you wake me - I would have liked that?"

She ignored my insincere protest. "I love this time of year - the long days and everything burgeoning. I like to get up early and not waste it."

"Have you had any breakfast?" I asked.

"No."

"Let me get you some."

While we were eating, I asked about the walk: where she had been, things she might have noticed, but she wasn't very forthcoming until we had started on our second cup of coffee.

"I've been doing a lot of thinking," she began. "It started before my walk, during the night."

"That sounds serious," I replied, almost saying 'ominous'. "What about?"

"About us, partly, but mainly about a decision I've got to make." I didn't ask, I just waited, and she continued: "There was an email for me when we got back. It was from Eric's daughter, Veronica. I think you'd better read it."

The letter was a long rambling one, full of bits of family news and problems; and I had to read it through again before I could pick up the main message and its implications.

Eric's house had been badly affected by the floods the previous January. This was something I recalled Linda mentioning some time before. The letter reiterated at length how his study and library had suffered a lot of damage. Friends and family members, including Veronica and her husband, had come to the rescue when they could, and had moved his possessions to the top of the house.

But, far more important to him than the harm to furniture and books was the disorder that had been produced during the rescue. Linda interrupted my reading to explain that, though his recent writing and research was all stored electronically, there remained the work of earlier years, embodied in stacks of paper in cardboard boxes. Much of this, we now learned, had been damaged by the water, only to be jumbled and scattered while being hastily gathered.

Veronica had helped her father as far as she could, but he really needed someone who understood the work to assist him in this huge retrieval task. So, please, could Linda, his old friend and one time assistant, spare some time to help?

I turned from the screen to look at her. "Are you going to?"

"I'm still making up my mind."

"Where does he live? I don't think you ever told me. Can you commute there - or would you have to stay overnight?"

"I'd have to stay. That's what I used to do."

"It seems a bit of a cheek to ask you to. . ."

"It's Veronica who's asking, not Eric."

"Why don't you wait for him to ask?"

"He wouldn't - he's too proud."

"Well then, why should you?"

"For the sake of friendship."

"But you don't want to, do you? And you don't owe him anything."

"I know."

I was beginning to panic - I was due to be leaving for home in the next hour or so, but now I wanted time and space to cope with all this. I needed to stay another day, at least; but, while trying to think of a way of asking, I remembered I was supposed to be home the next day for an important meeting of the estuary conservation group. Important? Well, it was something I wouldn't previously have considered missing. But it wasn't just that: I was due to go to Essex to stay with my older daughter, Felicity, in two days time.

I don't know how long I sat there, staring at the screen, before Linda gently poked me. "There's no need to be jealous. He's not a young man - he's. . . seventy-nine!" She looked amused and that irritated me.

"Surely," I replied, "if it's that important he could ask you himself."

"You're calling me Shirley again. No, seriously, his asking or not asking me makes no difference. There are lots of things to consider - and I don't feel like talking about them just now."

"I'd better go and pack," I replied, eventually.

§

24

Mike is on a train, heading out of Wales. He is still feeling the after-effects - the racing heart and tight chest - of his having to run to the station carrying his luggage. But now he is recalling a different pain: the emotional violence of their parting row, unresolved because of the need to catch the train.

Mike is being passively herded with other squaddies through labyrinthine processes at the port of Harwich, before ending up in the hold of a troop ship. Finally, a welcome sleep within a forest of hammocks, surrounded by steel and the smell of paint.

Another train, this one traversing Holland. He is getting used to the panic and helplessness he feels whenever he thinks of the increasing distance that separates them. Going AWOL, that earlier release from desperation, is no longer possible. Out of the window, the landscape sometimes looks homely, sometimes strange. All those level crossings with crowds of waiting cyclists. Later, after a sleep, he contemplates miles of featureless woodland. Have they reached Germany yet? No-one else in the carriage seems to know. His companions are playing cards and they invite him to join them. At some point the game finishes. He takes out the book that Linda bought him for the journey and escapes into the strange but benign universe of a story by Isaac Asimov.

For much of the drive home I fumed and fretted at myself for not having found a way to stay longer. I hadn't got any pet animals that needed looking after; it wouldn't really have mattered if I had missed that meeting; and I could have gone straight to Essex, topping up any clothing needs by shopping on the way, or when I got there.

I stopped twice with the intention of calling Linda on my mobile but each time I just couldn't bring myself to talk. Eventually, I sent a text message: the single word "sorry".

I had calmed down by the time I got home and I phoned her right away.

"How was your journey?" was the first thing she said.

"Not bad. Rain in places, as they used to say on the weather forecast." I didn't listen to what she said next - I was too impatient to ask, "Well, have you made up your mind?"

"Yes."

"So, what have you decided?"

"To go and help Eric."

"I guessed you would."

Our conversation finished soon after that but, about 10.00pm - I had just turned in for an early night - she called me to ask how I was. Her voice was its old self - no longer tight and frosty - and we soon seemed reconciled. She talked about her pessimism, her forebodings about going back to work with Eric, even for a short time. But she stressed how bad she would feel if she didn't help him.

While she was recounting the thinking, the weighing up she had done on her solitary walk, I remembered something else she had said - and felt a little cold lump of unease, somewhere in my chest. I waited until she had finished before I spoke of it: "When you came back from your walk you said you'd needed to think about things. When I asked 'what things', you said 'about us', but then you only spoke of the decision concerning Eric. What did you mean by 'about us'?"

I waited. She replied eventually, "Oh, I was just thinking about. . . what we might be doing in the future." She didn't want to talk about it any more just then.

The next day I was busy enough to forget my unease at her

reply. The meeting went well. I was able to help with the final arrangements for the summer timetable of guided walks on the salt marshes and seashore. I would be taking part on certain days in July and August. Apart from wondering briefly how long she intended staying at Eric's, I hardly thought of Linda during the day. It was in the evening that I found her email waiting for me.

It began by confirming that she would be travelling, by bus, to Eric's house the following day. Then, after giving me his address and landline number, she wrote:

Please forgive this being an email. I was going to send you a proper hand-written letter but I'm short of time. I thought of phoning, but I had misgivings about that - I need to be reflective, and to consider my words carefully to avoid misunderstandings.

When you first visited me, all our old feelings returned. We had found each other again, and there was the promise of new beginnings.

We both knew that our separation in the past had been the right thing. I had found John, you had found Margaret - the right partners for our lives - and we each understood the other's loss. We laughed about destiny having kept us both on the back burner for each other. It seemed right to use words such as 'destiny', even though I'm not sure if I believe in any such thing.

Anyway, for a time it all seemed wonderful and full of promise. Too good to be true. But since then things have cooled so quickly.

I can imagine what sensible people and relationship counsellors would say: that we should be grateful for the brief honeymoon time we had. Even if our adolescent passions can be rekindled, we shouldn't expect them to last for very long! And that leads me to ask what else have we got? - in common, and in the way of a future together.

I'm sorry if this sounds all clinical and psychological but I think what we originally had was a peculiar sort of love. A psychologist called Tennov wrote about the kind of intense, excessive love that can develop when it can't be fulfilled. It can arise when the lovers are separated, by distance, or by parents. (We suffered from both, at different times, didn't we?) The lovers are forced to live in a state of unrequited longing. If they are able to be together occasionally, as we were, that just makes it worse - it reinforces it. She called this kind of love 'limerence'.

We broke up while we were separated - when you were in Germany. Our feelings were still there, unresolved - 'unfinished business'.

I hope you understand - I don't want us to separate - this is not another 'Dear John' letter. But I want us to think about and talk about the future of our relationship - the loving friendship that we have.

After I've got my Eric work over and done with, maybe we could go away somewhere, together but on neutral ground, to see if we can work things out. . .

§

25

The little front garden was a cheerful thing to behold. The green of the shrubs and brilliant flower colours sang in defiance of the leaden afternoon sky and were unexpectedly heart-warming. I stood briefly to look at it, enjoying the scent of Wisteria blossom, before ringing the doorbell. While I waited I reflected on this one of many ways that Felicity took after her mother. I recalled how, from the age of six, she had always had her own piece of ground where she grew vegetables and flowers of her own choosing and how, apart from that chaotic time in her teens when everything went into abeyance, this interest had continued to grow and flourish. And then, after her marriage, she and Jim had done so much to develop and improve this ex-council house, the first and only home they owned. Maggie and I had often been impressed, when going to stay with them, to see how things had evolved since our previous visit.

Felicity opened the door dressed in blue jeans and an ochre-coloured canvas smock. "Dad!" We hugged. "Have you had any dinner?"

"Yes. I stopped for some food on the M4."

"That must have been hours ago - are you hungry?"

We went to the kitchen where she cut bread and warmed up some soup on the stove. I sat and talked to her while she worked, noticing how much her thin face had filled out since I last saw her. After I had eaten we went to sit in the room overlooking the front garden.

"When will the boys be home from school?" I asked.

"Anytime now. We'll see the bus go past the window."

We continued exchanging bits of news and talking about little things that never get included in phone calls.

Then she said, "When I first saw you at the door you looked a bit down in the dumps. Is everything all right?"

"It's driving long distances," I replied. "Too much time to think. I was remembering times long ago when you were little." It was true: I had been having what I call 'Margaret moments', or 'Maggie moments' if I'm referring to them lightheartedly; and I had been recalling very remote times, when we still lived in a flat and Felicity was our only child. For some of the drive, of course, I had been concerned with the present, and Linda.

She stood up and pointed to the window. "There's the bus." Minutes later the two boys appeared, in school uniform, and said hello before they disappeared up to their rooms, supposedly to do their homework.

Then Felicity asked, "Did you have a nice holiday. . . with Linda?"

"Yes, we did."

"Where was it you were staying?"

"Most of the time in North Wales. I think I told you, we went to stay with friends from my university days?"

"Oh, yes. But didn't you say it was an old school friend."

"It was both, in the case of Dennis."

"You've always liked Wales - you're not planning to move there, are you?"

"No. I haven't any plans for moving at the moment."

I wanted to drop the subject so I went to get my bag and take it up to my room. While I was upstairs I went to see my older grandson. He didn't seem to want to talk, being deeply involved with his computer. I asked what he had to do for homework and went across to look at the screen. The sounds, which I seem not to have noticed, should have given the game way: shoot'em up - move forward – shoot'em up. . .

"I thought you were doing your homework."

"Don't tell Mum!"

"Then do your homework, or I will."

"That's blackmail."

"That's right! So, what have you got to do?"

"Something boring."

"How about some details."

"Maths; and I've got to finish a history project."

I went to look in on his brother's room and found him sitting over books at his table but with the TV on. "I am doing my homework!" he protested. I asked him about it but met the same inability or unwillingness to talk. I remembered how much easier it had been to have a conversation with both of them when they were younger. I used to amuse them with silly jokes, and stories about what I got up to when I was their age.

Later that evening, sitting round the dining table, they were more forthcoming.

Two years before, they had all come to stay with me and we began to talk about the possibility of a similar visit towards the end of the summer holiday. It was gratifying to hear them say how much they had enjoyed it and how they were looking forward to coming again. Felicity put a slight damper on things by saying quietly to me, "You won't go taking them for dangerous walks on the cliffs, I hope, or letting them light fires." I just grinned. She had always been too risk-averse but I had given up arguing with her on that score.

The conversation turned to gardens and plants, then to places I might visit while I was there. I talked about the parts of Essex and Suffolk that I knew as a child and other places that Maggie and I went to with our daughters when they were children. I said how I'd begun to appreciate East Anglia even more since going to live in Devon.

"What made you leave this area?" asked Jim, a local man who wouldn't live anywhere else, even though he and Felicity liked to explore and holiday throughout the whole of the British Isles."

"Don't you remember?" Felicity replied for me, "Lucy had gone to live in Devon after she finished at uni. Sorry, Dad - *university* - I know the 'uni' word makes you wince. After a while, Mum and Dad decided to move there as well."

"I'd forgotten that," said Jim.

"And then," continued Felicity, her voice hardening, "Lucy ups and leaves you both to go and live in Birmingham. You must feel stranded now you're all alone."

"Do you think you'll ever move back here?" asked Jim.

"You were talking of doing so," put in Felicity before I could answer, "When you were staying with us, last summer. I think it's a good idea to move near one of us, now that you're. . ."

"Approaching middle age?" I managed to get in. They laughed; and the conversation moved elsewhere."

§

26

It was early morning when I heard the news. I almost missed it, weather reports only getting my attention when they refer to my area. But a particular place name had been mentioned and I was alerted enough to recapture it, to 'play back' the last few ignored words.

It was a report on rainfall and flooding in the West Midlands and one of the places mentioned was where Eric lived. I remembered the Shrewsbury floods of the previous January and this new situation sounded just as serious.

I tried phoning Linda. She was unavailable, probably at Eric's, so I tried his landline number. All I got were some strange noises and then silence, so I thought I would leave it for a minute or so and try again. While I waited I thought of Linda.

She had phoned me as soon as she arrived at Eric's house the first time. Since then we had spoken very little - just a couple of short calls while I was at Felicity's and at odd times subsequently. She always kept me informed about her trips to Eric's house and her short stays there but she ignored my attempts to get her to talk any further about us and our future. The emails we exchanged were more satisfactory for some reason. They left me with a feeling that she still thought of us as having a future, but needed to concentrate on what she had gone there for. As she'd put it: any talk now about our relationship would only distract her and undermine her resolve to stick with the work. It was now getting towards the end of June, and she was still saying how difficult she was finding the Eric work, now that her heart wasn't in it.

I phoned again but with no success. I then called her mobile number but the call failed to be sent. I tried again with a text message. This time I was successful and she replied shortly afterwards:
With Eric, cut off, road flooded, landline out, emerg servs aware
I texted back to say I was on my way.
In reply I got, *Stay home, nothing u can do. X*

I remained sitting where I was in a sort of paralysis, wondering if my empty, irrational offer to go there came from a genuine impulse, or was it just a knee jerk bit of bravado? After all, what *could* I do?

It was as though it was someone else that suddenly got up and began gathering things. There was no real sense of 'ought'; and I certainly didn't want to go on that journey.

I started making a list, but ended up just getting things and packing them into the car as they came to mind. Waterproof clothing, waders, plenty of cash from the nearest ATM - I had no idea where or for how long I would be staying. I told my next-door neighbour where I was going and then set out. An old TV news item popped into my head - a picture of boats being used in flood rescue. I turned around and went back to pick up my inflatable canoe, pump and paddles. It seemed silly but you never know, I thought; it might come in useful.

Once I was on the North Devon Link Road, heading for the M5, I calmed down. Plenty of time on the journey to think about what to do when I arrived. I then began to feel daunted by the vagueness and uncertainty of my mission. I remembered with relief that the OS Explorer map of that area was still in the car from the previous trip. I put on some soothing music and planned as far as I could what to do when I got there. Where was 'there' exactly? And how close could I actually get?

The real problems started in the afternoon after I left the M54 near Telford. The rain had stopped and the floods and diversions so far had been easy to cope with. But then I got caught in the sort of situation I had been dreading. A road was closed and the diversion, along a narrow track way, was being used by vehicles going both ways. It was blocked by two lorries trying to pass each other, and I was soon being buried deeper and deeper from both directions. I got out of the car and walked about, talking with other drivers to keep my spirits up. Then I tried calling Linda on Eric's landline number; and this time I got through.

It was she who answered and I hardly recognised her voice. My first impression was that she was angry with me but it was desperation I was hearing. As soon as I told her I had disobeyed her, and that I was now stuck, only a few miles away from her, she laughed and said, "Serves you right - you must be mad." Then followed questions and descriptions in no logical order of priority.

She started by mentioning the trouble with the landline which, as I obviously knew, was now working again. She apologised for being 'minimal' in her text messages - the mobile had to be saved for important things. "I can't recharge it - we've got no electricity." I started to ask about charging it from the car but she interrupted to say there were no cars - she had gone to Eric's by bus and his car was elsewhere, his daughter, Veronica, having been using it just before the road was cut off. I then asked how they were managing without electricity and she explained that they had gas for cooking and candles and an oil lamp for lighting. "Thank goodness it's summer and the days are long." It only occurred to me then to ask if they were in actual danger. She replied, "Not so far, but it's getting worse;" and then went on to describe the situation:

"Yesterday the road in front of the house disappeared. It's under a big lake that used to be fields. Our driveway is still there - it slopes up towards the house, but that's gradually disappearing. The rain has stopped but the water is rising everywhere. What worries me - and Eric, but for different reasons - is the back of the house. . ."

"Why?" I interrupted. "Is Eric coping? I noticed it was you who answered the phone."

"He's not much help. I can speak freely - he's currently rescuing things that are important to him so that we can get them into the loft. I was telling you about the rear. The house backs on to the hillside. I don't know if there's a name for this design but it's two storeys at the front, while at the back it's one storey - looks like a bungalow from behind. I'm worried because water is pouring off the ground behind us and hitting the back wall. So far, it's just cascading round the side but I'm worried it's going to break in."

While we were talking, the police had arrived and somehow - I failed to see how - had partly cleared the blockage. A policeman was vigorously waving me on and I rushed to get into the car. The wheels spun before I managed to get going through the brown slurry.

§

27

I took a chance and put my foot down, accelerating through the pool in the road - ten feet long and goodness knows how deep. Then I continued in low gear up the hill, the near side wheel fighting the torrent that was feeding the pool. Somewhere near the summit I found a place to stop. Next to a field gate, set back on the left, was a patch of muddy grass where I could park off the road.

I ate the last sandwich and a chocolate bar while I studied the map through a magnifier, eventually finding the tiny rectangle that should be Eric's house. I then got out of the car and went through the gate to look down the grassy slope to where the field became a lake. In the distance the ground rose again and I could see a line of trees. With the aid of my binoculars I could make out two buildings. I checked the map. The house I was seeking was one of three. I looked again. Yes! There was a third among the trees. Time to phone Linda.

While waiting to be answered I wondered what I would say if it was Eric who spoke. But it was Linda again.

"Nearly there!" I declared with too much enthusiasm. "I'm parked in a place that should be just a mile or so from you. I haven't got a compass to check if the direction is right but I can see a house that could be the one."

She didn't reply for a few seconds but then said in a dull voice that reminded me what she must be going through, "Congratulations. But you won't be able to reach us. So near yet so far, isn't it?"

"Don't be so pessimistic," I said. "Listen. I want you to help me confirm that I've got the right house in sight. From the contours, and what you told me about the place, I must be looking towards its front. I'd like you to wave something conspicuous from one of the upstairs front windows."

She snorted, then laughed and agreed to comply.

After five minutes of staring through the binoculars, with eyes blurring and watering, I was about to conclude I had made a mistake when I caught sight of a movement in the right place - something flickering rather than waving. It wasn't conclusive enough so I called her again.

"Did you wave? I thought I saw something but couldn't be sure."

"I had a better idea," she replied. "I poked Eric's big umbrella with its black and white panels out of the window and twirled it."

"So that's what I saw! - it looked like a magpie. Right - I'll see if I can get to you."

My confidence - soon to fade - arose from the plan I had been working on while waiting for her signal. I would get out the canoe and try to reach her by paddling across the 'lake'. The car could be safely left - it was on high ground, in as good a place as any around there. I told her what I intended.

"Can you do that?" She then began to protest about futile risks. I rang off quickly.

The canoe was fully inflated. It was then, while deciding what I should or could take with me, that exhaustion and despair descended. The sun, having been out in the afternoon and some of the evening, was now behind thick cloud; and the landscape was looking dark and big and threatening. All that water; and beneath it would be tree stumps and branches and posts and goodness knows what other hazards, all capable of tearing the fabric. Could I paddle all that distance? Was I going to be in actual danger? I stood unsteadily, looking at the sky. No time for rest - in spite of the long June day it was now well and truly evening and, if I didn't go now, what would I do?

I set out wading, trying not to slip, through the shallow water on the lake fringe, pushing the canoe. Eventually, I reckoned it was deep enough to get in and paddle. My first attempt was unsuccessful and I tipped over, getting drenched. I wasn't too bothered, knowing from experience that I would be getting wet in various ways; the mere act of using a double paddle causes water to trickle down your arms. I had managed to keep the rucksack and contents dry.

Once I got moving, the familiar rhythmic action began to make me feel stronger and less exhausted. So far, no snags - they might come when the water became shallow again.

Ten minutes into the crossing things were not so good. My arms and back had begun to ache and my bum wasn't comfortable. I endeavoured to overcome this with positive perceptions. After all, cutting through water with neither current nor waves was relatively easy; and the smooth surface was showing up a pronounced, satisfying bow wave that gave an encouraging impression of speed. Anyway, I knew I just had to keep going until the water became shallow again.

§

28

I was lying, eyes closed, in a warm bath. Dry clothes were to hand and there was promise of hot food to follow. This moment of bliss was to be savoured. The only discomforts were the sore leg, torn when getting over the partly submerged fence at the end of my voyage, and the pain in my forehead from having struck it when I slipped on the slimy front step.

I opened my eyes and looked out the bathroom window. 'Crepuscular' was just the right word to describe the scene - the last faint trace of summer evening light from the window plus that from a single candle in the room.

Success! I had actually found my way to the house. My daft, thoughtless intention of coming to Linda's rescue had born fruit. Or had it? I began to feel doubtful, a bit foolish. In what way could my being there actually help? I had brought a small supply of food in my rucksack, but it wasn't needed - early flood warnings had prompted Linda and Eric to stock up with essentials. All the 'rescuing' in this sense had been done by Veronica who, living nearby, had been able to come round and help out by doing shopping trips in Eric's car until she was finally prevented from reaching the house. And there was still the threat of the rear wall collapsing. I hadn't yet asked about that.

My euphoria, like the bath water, was cooling rapidly so I reluctantly got up to begin drying myself. Some stiffness in my back, chest and arms but no pain as yet - that would probably strike tomorrow. I glanced to where the clothes had been placed. They should easily fit me, Eric being at least my height and a bit broader.

Eric - the legendary Mr Casaubon! - had met me at the front door, along with Linda, the two of them helping me up from where I had fallen. His appearance was quite different from what I had pictured: taller, with a pale face that was smooth and young for his age. Linda once mentioned he had a beard and I imagined grizzled stubble; but he sported a neat white 'Colonel Sanders' with matching moustache.

After I had dressed I made my way to the stairs, taking my candle with me and catching sight of myself in a mirror on the landing. Old jeans, check shirt, jumper - loose and comfortable. Appetizing smells of food now made me aware of how hungry I was.

The kitchen was lit by an oil lamp and several candles. Lack of electricity had not been too much of a problem because, as Linda had already explained, the house had gas - the cylinders were outside, round the back and not yet under water - as well as a solid fuel stove. Hence the unexpected hot bath and hot food.

While I ate they answered my questions and brought me up to date. It was now too dark to inspect the waterfall at the rear. The rate of flow had gone down a bit and, so far, the wall was holding up. The water at the front had only risen enough to cover the front garden and lap over the doorstep - unlike in January when the whole ground floor, including Eric's study and library, had been flooded and wrecked. As I already knew, his furniture, books, papers and equipment had been moved to a room upstairs while the place was being refurbished. Now he was anxious because this new study was under threat - the room being the endangered one at the back. He had been struggling to get as much stuff as he could from there into the loft. I offered to help, recognising a way in which I could be of use. I now understood Linda's previous wry comment about Eric rescuing things that were important to him. He wasn't so concerned about the furniture and general belongings as he was about the books, computer stuff and things to do with his writing. This was something I could understand. At one point, an alarming thought occurred to me: was there any likelihood of the *whole house* collapsing, loft and all, if the wall gave way? Eric seemed confident there was little chance of that because it wasn't a supporting wall.

They sat at the kitchen table with me while I ate. I couldn't see their faces clearly in the dim light but their stressed condition and weariness was obvious in the way they both seemed slumped and in the way they spoke. Sometimes I could hear the sound of flowing water and every time I was reminded of the situation at the rear I felt anxiety. But they seemed inured, fatalistic about it and, in time, I went along with them. I wanted very much to ask all sorts of things about the situation but they clearly had no energy left for conversation.

The time came when there was talk of turning in, trying to get some sleep. "I don't mind staying up for a while," I offered, "to keep watch. . .be vigilant. . . in case of anything happening." Eric thought there was no need but I said I would anyway. "I'll give you a hand tomorrow," I said, "moving stuff into the loft - or whatever else you need."

Shortly after that I went upstairs to the bathroom and met Linda, just going into her room. I stopped her and whispered, "When I told you I was coming, and when I spoke to you on the way, you seemed a bit sharp with me. I don't blame you - I'm not much use here. I'm just another mouth to feed."

"Don't be daft." she replied, "I was worried about you, that's all. I'm glad you're here."

"So, my turning up wasn't completely unwelcome."

The candlelight was bright enough for me to see her smile. "What do you think? My young soldier - well, not so young, but just as reckless, coming to rescue me. I'm impressed." She went in and closed the door. I returned to the kitchen to begin my vigil.

29

Back into the dream; but this time with an awareness of having already been there, so I resist. There are strong rhythms in that dream: I am paddling the canoe, although from my swollen soft palate I think I've also been snoring. My body longs for more sleep but it is also in pain from its cramped position in the armchair by the kitchen stove. There is light outside and that motivates me to get up.

The first thing that occurred to me was to go outside to see if I could find a way round to the back of the house and look at the situation. The front door opened just as I reached it and Eric came in, carrying a spade and a pair of wellingtons. He looked very spry and capable, considering his age.

"Is it going down?" I asked.

"Not much."

"Anything I can do to help?"

"Not at the moment - after breakfast. I just got a message from Richard, my son-in-law. He's managed to get hold of a boat, and he's hoping to get here, sometime this morning with any luck."

"Oh, good. I was about to go and have a look round the back to see if there was anything I could do."

"Nothing can be done about that." He began to explain. I found his resignation, his obduracy and lack of emotion a bit worrying. Then he said, "Come upstairs, you can see what it's like from there."

By leaning out of a window in the very room that was under threat, I could see a smooth, slick-like flow of ochre-coloured water, cutting a channel between the wall and the bank. From that angle I couldn't see exactly how deep it had become, but it seemed to me that the threat was no longer of just the back wall being breached, but of the house itself being undermined. I was reluctant to comment on this in case Eric's stoicism - now reassuring - was also undermined, but I eventually spoke up. He said he was confident that the foundation, buried in the hillside, could take it; and he added, to my further relief, that the flow rate was lower than it was yesterday.

Back in the kitchen, seeing Linda by daylight, I noticed how tired she looked. She wasn't inclined to talk so I just helped as I far as I could with getting breakfast. There seemed to be plenty of everything we needed except for bread, which had run out the previous day. After breakfast I helped Eric by carrying box files and stacks of psychology journals up into the loft. Then, at about 11.00, I heard voices at the front door.

Richard's arrival, the introductions, and the down-to-earth talking that followed soon began to have a relaxing, cheering effect which I could see in Linda's and Eric's faces as well as feel myself. As well as being young and robust looking, Richard was reassuringly optimistic about everything. Appropriately, a minute after he turned up, the electricity came on. We all cheered. Eric and I then went out to help bring in the items he had brought.

After we had finished unloading I talked to Richard - asking about how far he'd had to travel by water and whether he had encountered the sort of problems I had. While he spoke I looked at the boat where he had beached it on the front lawn - now visible. It was only about eight feet long but just what was needed with its tough glass-fibre hull, flat bottom and small outboard motor.

He related some details such as having to get out and tow when the water was too shallow and how, in spite of his being careful, the propeller had become fowled by vegetation, stalling the motor. He'd had to use a paddle for the last fifty yards or so. His face then took on a pained expression as he said. "I scraped it on a submerged fence post, just over there - a concrete one, I think. Now it leaks. It doesn't belong to me - I borrowed it from a neighbour. It's the - what do you call it? - tender, belonging to his yacht."

Linda came out to join us. In spite of the warmth of the midday sun on that south facing side of the house, she obviously felt cold: she was huddling inside an outsize Barbour coat belonging to Eric; and she looked frail and wan.

After we'd had a meal at about 3.00 - mainly from items that Richard had brought - it was time for him to leave. While he talked to Eric, I waited to go out with him to the boat, to give him a hand getting under way. Just as he was about to leave I heard him ask, "Have you got a small saucepan or something I can use as a baler?"

"I can fix you a better baler than that," I said, and I headed for the kitchen where I remembered seeing a four-pint plastic milk bottle in the fridge. I poured the milk into a jug and replaced the cap. Then I took a sharp knife and cut off the bottom at an angle. "Here," I said, handing it to Richard, and trying not to show too much satisfaction at being able to help in this small but essential way.

§

30

There were no serious problems on that short journey, two days later, from Eric's to Linda's. We had woken up that morning to find the road outside Eric's house to be almost clear of water. I went for a long walk to see if the adjoining roads were also unblocked, and if it was possible to reach my car. I had pictured it to be somehow lost in mud but there it was, surprisingly clean and dry; and it started first touch. Three hours later, I had loaded it with our belongings and the deflated canoe.

The peril had passed: the once menacing cascade was now just a trickle and Eric declared confidently that, even though serious work needed to be done as soon as possible to shore up the bank, there was no immediate danger of collapse. Several people - neighbours, friends and relations - turned up during the day to help in different ways. They all seemed so young and capable; and suddenly it looked as though there was nothing more that Linda or I could do. Before we left I spoke to Eric, to commiserate and express how appalled I felt at his rotten luck in having the house wrecked by flooding, not once but twice. He thanked me, but said little in reply.

Once we had begun our journey I asked Linda, "What is he going to do now? You were just going to tell me about his short-term plans when you were called away to do something or other."

"He's going to stay with Veronica and Richard for a bit. And he may rent a cottage somewhere - I heard him telling them about it. He's going to put most of his furniture into storage while the house is being sorted. He wants to get out as soon as possible."

"That's understandable!"

As we arrived, I remembered the reason for her going to Eric's in the first place. "Were you able to help much with his writing?"

She shrugged. "I'd done a lot of editing, before all the bother, and I managed to transcribe some of his longhand notes on to computer before the power went, and to get the rest into some sort of order." Then she added, putting on a face of exaggerated weariness, "If he ever gets to the end there's going to be a big problem with the bibliography."

As soon as we'd unloaded and got into the house we both just flopped. All I recall of the rest of the day are a takeaway, some wine and an early night.

Next morning, we were standing side by side in bright hot sunshine in the conservatory. I had woken up thinking about our relationship and I was keen to get on to that subject, but it didn't feel like a suitable time and I couldn't find a way to begin. Still, there was no urgency - I wasn't due to go home until the afternoon.

But something else urgent then came to mind. "Sweetheart, do you mind if I use your computer?"

"Of course not. Is it for emails? By the way, you haven't phoned your daughters to say we got back safely."

"Yes, one email: I want to write about our adventure for my diary, and send it to myself."

"Your diary? You don't keep a diary."

"Yes I do."

"But you were bemoaning the fact that you had no diaries to aid your memory, as well as no photos. You cheekily asked to read mine and I wouldn't let you."

"That was just diaries in the past. I'm trying to keep one now - a properly written, detailed one.

"Mm. . . that's interesting. I wonder what you've been writing about us?"

"I might let you see, one day." This was the moment, but before I could speak she continued:

"Friends tell me it's hard to get into the diary habit in later life, if you've not been used to it. Have you been writing it regularly?"

"Not regularly. But I've written quite a lot since I started."

"When was it you started?"

"Last summer. It all began when I noticed a scent." I was suddenly distracted by the return of the memory of that day.

"Well, go on."

I asked, "Do you remember the name of a rather sweet perfume you used to like back in the 1950s?"

She paused to think, then shook her head. I went on to summarise the chain of events that had led to our being together. Then, after looking thoughtful again, she said, "It could be one called *In Love* - I used to like that."

"That's the one!" I said, clumsily putting my arms around her. "I remember buying you some as a present." I pulled her closer and kissed her. She responded for a time but her heart wasn't in it. I didn't comment. I then went off to her study to write my diary-email.

By the time I had finished it was midday. I stood up and went to look for Linda.

She was in the kitchen, preparing lunch, so we continued our previous conversation, sitting at the table.

"You know," I began, "your querying my diary writing made me think about it, and I connected it to my *compulsion*, as you call it, to photograph everything. I think I know where it comes from."

"And that is?" she said, while I drew a breath.

"The fact that for much of my life I've been disregardful of the present. When I was at school I was constantly fantasising about the future, always looking forward to when life would be good. The good time came during early married life, especially when the children were young. And then I was too happy - and too busy - to be bothered with writing about it. Later, after a few of life's disappointments, I began to look back with nostalgia to those times, and other periods in the past. This was particularly the case after Margaret died. Throughout my life I've lived the present but never taken much notice of it. Nowadays, people video and photograph everything, especially since digital cameras came along. They have hundreds - thousands - of images on their computers. And, now that I'm trying to be more aware and mindful of the precious present, I want to record it."

She said nothing so I asked, "Well, does that make any sense?"

"It makes sense," she replied eventually, "but it also reminds me of something Dennis told me when we were there. It was while you were fussing with your photos. He said how he once felt compelled to photograph beautiful things - nature, landscapes, animals. But he learned that trying to grab images got in the way of looking at them properly, of contemplating them."

"Well, yes," I said," but a photo saves the image for you to look at later, any number of times."

"But the original experience has been impoverished. He stressed how you need to look at things; and he went on to say that it was when he drew things or painted them that he really looked at them properly and got to know them."

"I'll bear that in mind," I replied, suddenly wanting to change the subject. I had just realised that I would be leaving soon and that we still hadn't got round to talking about our future.

I eventually managed to find what felt like a good moment, but Linda declared that she was reluctant. "I'm feeling much too tired, really exhausted," she said. "I want to get my thoughts and feelings together properly. I'll send you a letter - an email - but not until tomorrow."

31

As soon as I got home I phoned Linda to tell her I had arrived. It was a very short conversation.

Over the next few days we went back to our custom of phoning mornings and evenings. We exchanged news of our families and of our health - we had both come down with a cold. We talked of everyday, domestic things. There was some humour but no banter, none of the old affection in our talk; and the fact that this didn't seem to bother me began to bother me. Often we seemed to be searching for things to say to each other. I caught myself describing in detail - too much - some work I was involved with for the Devon Wildlife Trust.

I thought about the promised email but didn't remind her. Eventually, it arrived:

> *Dear Mike,*
>
> *I'm sorry I've been so long in writing this letter, the one I promised.*
>
> *It's been hard. I didn't want to hurt or discourage you unduly because I believe we <u>could</u> have a future together, once we've got through this strange wintertime in our feelings.*
>
> *What a contrast - It was pure joy to rediscover each other, to feel that young love (not to mention young lust) coming to life again. And it was wonderful getting to know you as the person you are now, after 50 years.*
>
> *But I don't feel right about the way things have developed since those heady first days. It's partly to do with <u>my</u> feelings about us - there's something missing. But my intuition tells me loudly it has to do with <u>your</u> feelings for me - I can't make them out.*

There was more, but it said much the same thing.

I quickly wrote a reply. It was a mess. I almost didn't send it; and then, after I did finally send it, I omitted to save it! I had been feeling indignant and slightly irritable as I wrote it. I suggested that, with her knowledge of psychology, she might be able to find and express a clearer explanation of the way things had gone. She might take this as sarcasm but I didn't care.

The next day I got another email from her. She had taken me at my word.

> *Dear Mike,*
> *So you want me to psychologise about us. Well, here goes:*
>
> *When you came to my rescue it felt really lovely - like a re-awakening of the old Mike I knew half a century ago. But the Mike of the noughties isn't just different - he's a bit of a contradiction.*
>
> *You've said that you <u>think</u> lovingly of me and that you <u>feel</u> affection for me. But, are you aware that you don't always <u>behave</u> as if you love me?*
>
> *Many things in our nature have these three aspects - the cognitive, the affective and the behavioural. People can be inconsistent in the ways they think or feel towards someone or something. Sometimes there's no connection between what they believe and how they behave - and it's this that I've been picking up from you.*
>
> *At the start of our new relationship you were making declarations of love - <u>protestations</u> of love. But later you seemed to change, and the way you've been acting towards me doesn't connect to the person you were at the start.*
>
> *I don't really understand my own feelings, either. I may be projecting all sorts of things on to you.*

> *However, please understand that I don't want us to make any hasty decisions about our future. I just think we need to be patient and see how things go.*
>
> *Let's leave things for a while - to settle. Then we could go for a short holiday somewhere. Nothing fancy - just a small hotel or B&B, somewhere we'd both like. Neutral territory, as I suggested before.*
>
> *How about sometime in late July or August? (Whatever fits in with your Wildlife Trust arrangements.) I'm free until September. As I told you, that's when I'm going away with Hayley & family.*

I sent her a short acknowledgement; and then turned to look, joylessly, through my calendar.

§

32

I had spent much of the day leading an excursion near the mouth of the estuary. Sharing the tuition was my friend Ken, who, before he retired, used to teach biology. He had the group studying the rock pools and digging in the mud and sand for invertebrate animals while I dealt with the plant life.

It was a warm July day. The weather was dull but good enough and we found examples of most of the species to be expected. After the group had looked at the green, red and brown seaweeds and collected a few specimens, we went on to discuss seaweed uses in medicine, cosmetics and cookery. We found some *Porphyra*, the sort used for making 'laver bread' but unfortunately there wasn't enough to make it worth gathering. In compensation I was able to bring them to a large spread of marsh samphire; and the free food enthusiasts, including myself, went about collecting some of that.

As soon as I got home that evening I checked my emails. Nothing from Linda but, to my surprise, there was one from Dennis. The main part was in the middle:

You remember I was telling you about the group from our school - the 'Old Stowfordians'. Well, it's time for the next annual get-together. Is there any chance you could come with me? I know you said before that you weren't interested, but I'm hoping you might change your mind. It isn't until next weekend - so, don't complain that I'm not giving you plenty of notice.

> *I'm asking you for selfish reasons. Gwen has gone with me before but this time she can't, and I'd like you to take her place. As well as the prospect of enjoying your company, I would appreciate having someone to help keep me awake on the journey, and perhaps share the driving.*
>
> *It's a sort of dinner with dancing (don't worry, you won't have to dance with me). We might have called it a 'social' in our days.*
>
> *I normally stay with my sister's family, not far from the venue. I have taken the liberty of asking them if you can stay with me, and they are quite happy about it.*

He went on to give me details of the venue: near Basildon in Essex.

My first response was my usual antipathy at the thought of having anything to do with the school; but later in the evening, after thinking about it and finding I was free around that time, I felt tempted. It might be interesting, even fun. I phoned him to say I would consider it and we went on to talk it over and work out travel details.

Further phone calls the next day led to it being settled. I would go by train to Birmingham. I had already been talking to my daughter, Lucy, about seeing her sometime soon, and I would stay at her place overnight. Dennis would pick me up the next day and we would drive down to Essex. On the way back he would leave me at Lucy's and then I could spend some proper time with her before going home by train.

I was in two minds about the trip: partly looking forward to it, but with a feeling of having been talked into going. The way it all seemed to work out was making me feel uneasy.

I talked to Linda on the phone later in the evening - I forget which one of us called the other. When I told her of my decision to go with Dennis she sounded very pleased on my behalf. "You'll enjoy that," she said. "I'm not so sure," I replied. I reminded her how those schooldays had not been a time of happiness, in contrast to my days as a university student, 'when I met my first love'. "Don't be such an old pessimist!" was her response. "Just think how interesting it could be."

Then she went on to talk about Eric:

"He's planning to move as soon as he can. Once the flood damage has been put to rights he intends selling. He's hoping to find somewhere in Worcestershire, near where his son lives. At the moment he's working like mad to downsize the library and clear out all those old journals and other stuff."

"The disaster seems to have concentrated his mind," I commented.

"Absolutely! He's now going all out to finish the history. Oh yes, and he's got someone else now to do the secretarial and editing work. She's someone he knows from way back - the wife of an ex-colleague. . ."

"I bet he's paying her!"

"Yes, he is. But please don't be nasty about that. I've been thinking about him recently. Imagine what it was like to go through what he has. He stood to lose so much; you know what his work means to him. Now he's much older than when I first knew him, I worry about his health and state of mind."

§

33

It was afternoon, and I was with Dennis at his sister's house, sitting outside on the patio. We were looking at old school photos - a few yellowing black and white originals, but most obtained by him from the Old Stowfordians' website. He had given me a copy of one of my old fourth year class. My own original had been lost or thrown out years ago.

I was struck by the sense of immediate recognition the picture provided. After the first glance I experimented by looking away, visualising and trying to put names to the images. Then I stopped and looked at it properly. Dennis held a copy of his class - 'Lower 5A' as opposed to my 'Lower 5B'. I now remembered that we had been in different classes - what would now be called 'tutor groups' or whatever - before getting to know each other in the Sixth Form.

I proceeded to name as many as I could from the array, making another discovery about memory for those familiar but oddly remote faces. It seemed to be all or none: I either knew the names - both first and surnames - or I didn't. There was no half remembering or getting it wrong. I commented on this to Dennis. He agreed about it but didn't seem very interested.

Then we swapped photos and did the same thing, prompting each other where there was a gap in memory. Mostly I had an 'of course!' reaction to being given the name although sometimes I recognised the face while the name meant nothing.

There were two faces in Dennis's class that I recognised as connecting with my unpleasant feelings about school days.

This prompted me to ask him if he knew who might be at the gathering.

"Goodness knows," he replied. "They won't just be from our year, of course."

"Well, show me the ones from our classes that have been to these functions before."

He picked out four, including one of the two I had noticed.

I then went back to looking at the photos and reminiscing. There was my old friend Pete from Years 2 and 3. He and I used to get up to all sorts of science activities, mainly at his house. I recalled that I had also known him in our primary school days when we used to make gunpowder. There was another friend, also called Pete; we used to go fishing together. I had kept in touch with him during National Service.

I looked at the two faces with unhappy associations. One was a boy whose name neither Dennis nor I could recall. He had been a bully - not the classical, cowardly loner of stories but a socially clever manipulator who knew how to get the crowd to be on his side. The other was a girl I went out with briefly before she dumped me.

Dennis then handed me some photographs of school drama productions. These included both serious plays and Christmas pantomimes. I caught sight of myself in one, looking tense and awkward.

At about 7.00 that evening Dennis and I, wearing suits and ties, were standing in a bar surrounded by an assortment of men and women of roughly our age. There was no-one I recognised. They all seemed friendly and eager to talk and, in no time, we were exchanging self-introductions, giving the years of our attendance, and talking about ourselves and any mutual acquaintances that came to mind.

As soon as we had sat down to eat I began to feel disappointed. I had been given to understand that the person who organised the seating arrangements had gone to great trouble to put us with people from our own or similar year but, apart from Dennis, there was nobody I recognised. There were eight of us around that table: four women, four men. I noticed that the woman to my right had a class photo in front of her. I leaned over to look and she smiled and handed it to me. I took a sip of wine and then picked it up. There it was again: the moment of sharp remembrance, the sense of deep familiarity. This was Lower 5C.

"I'm sorry," I said, "I can't place you."

"Dorothy Smith - now Dorothy Candler." She pointed to the photo - to a thin little girl with a large perm. She wasn't somebody I remembered and so, apart from the face on the photo, there was no image in my head to be mentally morphed into the woman sitting next to me. I showed her my class photo and pointed to myself. She had no recollection of me either.

"We all seem to have group photographs from the Fourth Year," I said. "Did they take any in the Fifth - that would be the final year for those who didn't stay on?"

"I don't know," she said. "They couldn't have taken any at the *end* of that year – we all cleared off as soon as our O Levels finished. No proms in those days."

That jogged my memory. "Do you remember the school dances?"

"Oh yes."

"We used to have a special one at the end of the summer term, didn't we? Some of the leavers used to come back for that."

That got us talking about the dances, the records that were played, the occasional benefit of a live band. Then the food arrived.

While we were on the puddings and cheeses, the woman on my other side spoke to me. "I've just remembered you. You weren't in my class but you were in my maths group in the Sixth Form."

I looked at her while I tried to recall doing A Level maths lessons. As soon as she told me her name I recalled a quiet, clever girl who was always coming top in the group. She told me about her subsequent career as a statistician and about her marriage. We had both been widowed at about the same time.

The band began to play a series of old dance tunes. I turned to look at the band members – very young men, playing tunes that would please the old fogies at the function. After they had played three or four numbers, the first couples began to get up and dance, although none of the people on my table showed any inclination to join in. Then I felt someone touch my arm; it was Dorothy Candler. "Would you like to dance?"

My first reaction was panic and demurral but I warmed to the idea now that there were more people dancing. It was a waltz, after all - difficult to botch completely unless I trod on her feet.

It eventually dawned on me how much I was enjoying the music and dancing.

One of the tunes hit the spot - it was one that we danced to at school; and it evoked that sense of excitement and promise that life can have when you're 16.

After we finished I remained standing. Dennis, who had not been dancing, was talking to a woman from another table. I drifted over to talk to them, curious to meet his companion. I had noticed her earlier and couldn't place her; I didn't think she was on any of the photos I had seen that day yet she looked familiar. Blue eyes and a shapely mouth set in a broad face, straight hair that had once been blonde, as I now vividly recalled. Of course! She had been in the Lower Sixth when I had been in the Upper.

"Hello Michael." That startled me - no-one now called me Michael.

"Hello. . . Jennifer." Fancied by all the boys in the Sixth and out of my league. We talked about our marriages and children. She had married the same boy she had gone steady with from school - someone from Dennis's class - and was still married to him. He was elsewhere in the room.

She suddenly said, "Will you dance with me, Michael? Old Dennis here is too cowardly, and my husband never did anything but jive in those days."

We danced to another old familiar tune - a quickstep. I was smiling at how I would have felt back then at being asked to dance by none other than *Jennifer*. Mind you, I had only been second choice after Dennis.

After we had danced we talked and I gradually got to meet a few more people from different years, including Jennifer's husband, George. After talking with George for a while, Dennis and I drifted back to our table to join the others there. A woman who had been sitting opposite me on the other side of the table came round to join us. She turned out to be someone from my own class. On hearing her name I recalled the girl on the photo, but it was impossible to see her in the very elderly-looking person in front of me. I managed to stop myself from blurting out about how much she had changed.

We talked about class members and various teachers. She spoke enthusiastically about memorably amusing characters among the pupils and staff. She reminded me about the 6th Form custom of wearing silly hats when running in the one mile race on sports day. Then she opened a large handbag and showed me some things she had downloaded from the web site. "Do you remember this?" she said, handing me three A4 sheets, stapled together. It was a modern printer copy of something ancient - typed and with cartoons.

"No?"

"It's that magazine, the newsletter that the 6th Form used to put together at the end of term."

Then I noticed the title: STOWFORD SCANDAL and recognised it.

"You can have it," she said. "I can print more copies."

"Thank you!" I folded it and put it in my pocket. Then I asked her if she would like to dance.

"Thank you but no," she replied. "My dancing days, such as they were, are no more."

We left at about 11.30 and travelled back by taxi. The event had energised me and I talked non-stop all the way. I must have tired Dennis out because when we arrived he made it clear that he wanted to call it a day and go straight to bed.

In my bedroom I was hanging up my suit when I remembered the newsletter in my pocket. As I unfolded it I caught sight of a little headline unnoticed before, at the top of the second sheet: 'La Ronde'. And I remembered.

I paused for several seconds before looking to see if it was what I feared. 'La Ronde' consisted of short reports about who in the Sixth was going out with whom, who fancied whom, who had split up etc. That was the time when I seemed to be the only one having no success in getting someone to go out with him. I was getting refusal after refusal - until I stopped trying, fearing I might be getting a reputation. Too late. I didn't need to look at that piece of paper to recall it speculating, *'Who is Germy's latest crush?'*

'Germy' had been the innocuous nickname I'd been given at age 13 - because 'Mike Rowe' sounded like 'microbe'. But I remembered too clearly how its use, now that I was 17, coupled with the word 'crush', had been humiliating - shaming.

The exhilaration I had feared would keep me awake gave way to unfocussed anger, then to tiredness. I slept surprisingly well that night.

§

34

One of the first things Lucy said, after greetings at the front door, was "Are you going to see Linda while you're here?"

"I thought about it," I replied, "but no - I'm not going to be here for very long."

It had occurred to me, on the road back to Birmingham, that while staying with Lucy I could take a day trip to Shrewsbury. It was odd that I hadn't thought of the possibility sooner; was it because I didn't really want to see her? I decided it wouldn't be fair to Lucy to go away during the short time I was there, even though I had done just that on the previous visit in January, and stayed away overnight.

Lucy looked good - same height as me, in heels, wearing a dark formal suit that set off her fair hair and skin. I complimented her. She shrugged, put on a mock scowl and explained that she had only just got in from work and hadn't changed back to her normal self.

I was soon sitting in an armchair looking out of a tall Victorian window at the evening sun shining through city trees. While we drank tea she explained that it would be just the two of us for most of the evening. Son-in-law Bill was playing tennis and wouldn't get in till about 10.00.

She asked about my health, just as she had during my brief stay before I went off to Essex. She always seemed unduly anxious about that. During Maggie's illness and after her death, Lucy was the one who had been able to come and stay with me and look after me. This had left her with a lasting tendency to fuss, as I saw it. When she came to stay she would take over, unless I could deflect her without upsetting her.

After a polite length of time following the tea, I mentioned that I was thirsty.

"What would you like?" she asked. "Some fruit juice?"

"How about a gin and tonic?"

"Oh, Dad! I thought you'd been sensible and given up alcohol."

"What gave you that idea? I know you wanted me to - and I did cut down a bit because you were so concerned." I omitted to say that I had reverted to my previous level.

Having got my own way I went on to describe what had taken place at the Old Stowfordians' dinner dance. She seemed delighted and reminded me that I had always spoken disdainfully of my grammar school days. She said how gratifying it was that I had enjoyed myself and changed my outlook.

"It helped to lay a few ghosts," I said.

A little later, while we were eating, I asked about Bill and how both their careers were progressing.

She was quick and dismissive in her replies, as usual. She has one of those new professions that didn't exist in my day and I can never got to grips with what exactly she does at work, in spite of her explanations.

She was keen to talk about Linda. "When are you going to bring her here to meet us? Sometime soon?"

I had difficulty giving a sincere answer. "I'm not sure when she can make it. She's due to go on holiday in September with her daughter's family."

"You've got the whole of August between now and then."

"Not entirely - Felicity was talking of coming to see me in August."

"Has she made a definite booking?"

"No, but. . ."

"Well then, I'm going to get in first!"

I laughed at this and said rashly, "No need! As soon as I know when they're coming I'll see what I can do about bringing Linda to meet you."

She gave me a 'knowing' look and said, "I have the impression you don't want us to meet."

I took a deep breath. "It isn't that. It's just that. . . things aren't quite right between us, at the moment."

"I felt there was something wrong."

"I used to think *you* were not keen on meeting *her*," I said defensively.

"Well, that was true for a while. When you first told me about Linda I thought she was just some old girlfriend. But then I remembered that bit of family history about you being sort of engaged while at university - although nothing came of it - and I realised she was the one. And then, even though you were careful not to say too much, I got a sense of how important she was to you, not just back then but now. And this horrible idea came to me that your marriage to our mum was just a sort of digression. . ."

"It isn't like that at all! Linda and I both know that we outgrew each other, and that we went on to marry the right people. It's just that, now we've lost the best, we're quite content to be each other's second best!" As I was saying this I felt a growing sense of doubt. Did this still apply to Linda and me? Had it all just been a short-lived romantic notion?

"I know," said Lucy. "You've already explained that to me. I was only telling you what I thought at that time. I don't any more. And that's why I feel better about you and Linda and want to meet her."

The next few days turned out to be a successful holiday and a welcome distraction. During the day I explored the city on my own, visiting museums, an art gallery and other similar places. In the evenings I enjoyed the company of Lucy and Bill. They even took me out - to the cinema and a theatre.

I sent Linda a couple of emails while I was there. The first was a cautiously worded version of my diary account of the dinner dance; the second, towards the end of my stay, told her what I had been doing in Birmingham. The email writing was very wearying and I really wanted to talk to her properly; however, I postponed phoning her until I got home.

§

35

Everywhere in town had that August look - the streets full of people in shorts and the shops full of inflatable beach toys, fishing nets and crab lines. I won't mention the traffic. As I walked back across the bridge to my home I was reminded again of the lack of any decision about where, and when, Linda and I would be going for our little holiday.

Later, in the early evening, I was doing odd jobs in my garden, looking occasionally at the estuary. It was low water and there was nothing of interest to be seen. I thought again about the holiday, and felt a rush of impatience and frustration as I realised how much I wanted to be with her. I went inside to look at my diary again. The following two weeks were clear of appointments and things that couldn't be missed or postponed. Now was the best time to go - I needed to talk to her again.

"The summer seems to be disappearing fast," I began. "Have you had any more thoughts about when we can get away together and where you'd like to go?"

It was several seconds before she answered. "I've got something to tell you. I was going to be a coward and leave it until I emailed you tonight but. . . I need to talk it over with you. It's about Eric. The work I was doing for him last time didn't get finished. The flood put a stop to it, didn't it. Well, he's asked me to go back and finish it."

"Oh. . ." I was impressed by my self-control. "I suppose that was to be expected. Well, he'll have to wait till we're back from our holiday, won't he."

"I'd rather get it over with first - otherwise it'll be a dreary old cloud hanging over me and spoiling things." She sounded quite miserable. "There isn't much left - it shouldn't take more than two days of concentrated work, three at most."

"I don't want to talk about this!" I replied. "Why can't he finish it on his own? It may take him longer that way but he doesn't *really* need you, does he?"

"Well, there are still lots of notes in my scribbly writing; and some of it's in shorthand."

My heart sank. There was no way I was going to talk her out of it - I'd got neither the arguments nor the energy. All I could say was, "I've been looking forward to being with you so much."

"Have you?"

"Yes, and I don't want to wait even a day longer than necessary."

After a pause she said, "I feel the same way, you know."

"But you want to go to Eric's first, don't you?"

"No," she said, with a touch of sharpness. "I'm very reluctant to go - it's just an unwelcome obligation. . . with problems."

"Problems?"

"Yes. I don't want to spend even one night in that house. It's a mess - there's building work going on, but it's not just that. I know I'd hate having to stay there overnight."

"So you'd go there daily - commute?"

"The trouble is, since the floods, the buses have been re-routed and it doesn't work out so conveniently."

"So you'll have to drive. . ."

"Will you please stop solving my problems for me and just let me talk!"

"Sorry."

"I've been trying to talk my own way through all this and I don't know what to do."

"You just don't want to go, do you."

"That's right. A state of conflict - I must, but I can't, but I must. . ."

Not knowing what to say next, I reverted to my rational questioning. "Is there a problem with driving there?"

"No more than usual I suppose."

"I don't understand."

"It's driving, isn't it. I get more and more nervous in traffic. Especially at night; and when the roads are wet."

"I didn't realise that." I thought back. "You drove us to that party in Wales, and that was at night."

"I don't mind country roads so much. Anyway, I was being nice to you. So you could have a drink - remember?"

I remembered, and felt guilty. "I'm sorry, I had no idea. . ."

"I'm not as badly off as Gwen - she can't drive at all now."

I reverted to problem solving: "If you do go this month, you won't be driving home in the dark." She didn't reply. "You're not thinking of giving up your car, are you?"

"Not yet. It's essential for some things."

She went on to say more but I didn't take it in. A solution had occurred to me - a very pleasing one. "Listen," I interrupted. "How does this sound? Let's postpone going away until later some time. How about if I come and stay with you for a few days. I'll drive you to Eric's and back each day. I can stay there while you're working, make myself useful; or I can get on with some reading. It'll be a holiday, of sorts. Well, what do you think?"

§

36

Shortly before midday, after spending most of the morning working with paper and computer, Linda said she had a headache and that she was going to take a break. She went off to have a stroll along the road leaving Eric and me in the study. I had been sitting in the kitchen, reading, keeping out of their way, concerned not to distract. I only happened to be in the room because I had just brought in yet another batch of coffee.

Eric had stopped working and I thought he might be wanting a rest himself. However, after several attempts at ordinary conversation I was getting nowhere. Then, just as I was about to go outside and join Linda, he suddenly deigned to give me some attention. He turned round towards me in his swivel chair and said, "Linda was telling me about your involvement with the wildlife trust. Has your area - the habitats and so on - been affected much by heavy rainfall?"

"To some extent - we've had a lot of wood and silt coming down the river. But we escaped actual flooding."

"Your background was in biology, wasn't it?"

"No, chemistry. Amateur ecology came later."

"Ah, I see. She also told me that you'd done some research in the history of science. What was that about?"

I summarised the topic for the M.Sc. His manner and relaxed attentiveness were encouraging and I was soon telling him more about my long-time interest in the matter. He wondered why I had never taken it further, into an academic career. Why indeed? I concluded it had to do with being sensible about career decisions and making a living. I made light of it: "I don't think I had the right kind of predilection to be a proper historian."

"You were a schoolmaster, weren't you?"

"No." I wondered what gave him that idea. "I worked mainly in industry as a laboratory chemist."

He smiled before saying, "Your reference to a 'proper historian' suggests you have some idea what history is supposed to be about. Am I right?"

"I don't know," I replied. "When I started on the M.Sc., I had to read a few things. One of them was R.G. Collingwood's *The Idea of History*. But not much else."

"I'm also intrigued," he said, "by your saying you didn't have - what was it you said? - the right predilection. What did you mean by that?"

I wasn't sure myself but I replied, "I think I meant my approach. I'd picked up enough about history as a discipline to realise that my liking for it was only that of the non-academic enthusiast. It was always the stories, the narratives, the evolution of the sciences that fascinated me."

His face lit up. "There's nothing wrong with that kind of predilection - we could do with more of it! To be entranced by narrative has been a part of my own motivation - and my weakness, the critics would say. My approach to the history of psychology is one that is often dismissed as celebratory and not sufficiently critical."

I recalled Linda using that word and I was about to say something when the lady herself came back into the room, her short hair looking spiky and wind-ruffled. Instead I asked, including her in the question, "What exactly are you working on at the moment?"

Eric glanced at her, as if to say "Go on - you tell him".

"The start of the Twentieth Century," she replied, "mainly in America."

I asked, "Would that include William James?"

"Well," she replied, "it includes some of his protégés." Eric nodded. She went on, "It's E. L. Thorndike at the moment and work with animals - the beginnings of the behaviourist movement."

"Will this be in the final volume?" I asked cautiously.

They seemed to exchange glances, and I wondered if I had put my foot in it.

It was Eric who replied: "No. This'll be in the last part of Volume Three, which finishes around 1914."

I remembered something and asked, "Linda once mentioned that you'd been thinking of recasting the work as a history of histories - is that still the case?"

Linda looked down. Had I embarrassed her by revealing too much of what she had told me?

But Eric smiled benignly, and then looked rueful. "That idea has long been abandoned." He sighed. "Recent events have brought home to me that I have to cut my coat to suit my cloth, as the saying goes." He suddenly turned his chair away from us to address his computer and begin typing rapidly.

"Come and help me get lunch," said Linda.

As soon as we were in the kitchen I asked her to give me the latest, if she could, on what his plans were towards finishing and publishing.

While we pottered about she explained, "Well, you heard him mention Volume Three. That's what we're embroiled with at the moment."

"What happened to Volume Two - did it get finished?"

"Yes, thank goodness. It's now being edited, and documented."

"By this new professional editor, I suppose."

"That's right. She's called Helena Ford."

"Have you met her?"

"No. She doesn't come here much - they work on line."

"You used the word 'embroiled' about Volume Three. Are things going badly?"

She nodded, and paused, while she rinsed and dried some lettuce. I took it from her and began to put the salad together. "The problem is," she continued in a voice lowered to a whisper, "he's anxious to get on with the last part - Volume Four. That's the big one that covers all the main developments of the Twentieth Century. She suddenly looked vexed. "He's urging me to get on with the outstanding work on Three, but he's being awkward about it - I've had to consult him every now and then, but he gets irritable and begrudges every bit of time and attention he has to give me."

My recent liking for Eric dissolved. He was once again the selfish, demanding, puffed-up old Casaubon. "What the hell does he want?" I exploded. "He expects you to help, without paying you, and then puts obstacles in the way!"

She clamped her finger to her lips and her eyes went wide with alarm. "Shh! He would pay me if I'd let him. He's only like that because he's so desperate to finish what he thinks is the most important part. I thought you understood. As you commented, the flood concentrated his mind. Well, it did more than that - it shook him up badly. He's been going on about how he must complete the work before he dies!"

An hour later we were sitting round the kitchen table eating our lunch in silence. The room was filled with bright daylight. It reminded me by contrast of my first meal in Eric's kitchen - the darkness, the candles.

As soon as the meal came to an end, Linda began gathering up the plates and cutlery. I was just about to stand up and find something useful to do when Eric started talking to me, continuing our earlier conversation. He began telling me how concerned he was to record and put into context his own work - the research area he was involved with before he retired. When I asked what this had been, he described it as 'human experimental psychology'. He used the phrase as if it had a very specific meaning and I asked if that was the name of a particular 'school' of psychology. He laughed, and said that nobody talks of 'schools' any more.

"Paradigms?" I suggested.

He grimaced. "I've lived and worked through a great deal of Twentieth Century university psychology. I have seen the so-called 'paradigm shifts'. I even remember the time when the word 'paradigm' meant something different, before 1962, when Kuhn hijacked the word."

"I suppose, when I started out, behaviourism was the paradigm for a lot of academic psychology, especially on the other side of the pond. But it went beyond animal work - its terminology permeated my human experimental research. It didn't just give us our vocabulary; it also gave us the framework and the tools. But, later, around the 60s, when a 'paradigm shift' was supposed to be occurring, and the term 'cognitive' was becoming flavour of the month, my colleagues and I realised we had been doing 'cognitive psychology' all along."

"It was the words that had changed: I had been researching 'verbal learning', and now I called it 'verbal memory'. Similarly, 'verbal behaviour' became 'language', and so on. Those who had been working on problem solving even began to use words like 'thinking'."

"It was computers and cybernetic ideas that were making the difference. When I started, we were making use of Information Theory. . ."

"Information processing?" I said.

"Not quite the same thing, but we also went there. Computer modelling and artificial intelligence were giving new approaches to old problems." He grinned. "And nowadays, with developments in neurobiology and brain imaging, we have researchers, once content to call themselves *psychologists*, now declaring themselves to be *cognitive neuroscientists*. Much more cool! He stood up and made for the door. "I must get back to work."

Something had crossed my mind and I called out, "Hasn't it been said that 'there's no period so remote as the recent past'?"

He stopped in the doorway and turned to me with a look of disapproval. Then he said, patiently, "Of course there's truth in that - for different reasons and different situations. Distance gives perspective. You have the benefit of the work of others. Also, if you're working on something remote from scarce primary sources then the greater the elapsed time, the greater the chance of finding access to more sources. However," he emphasised, "in the short term, distance also means *forgetfulness*."

"I can see that," I replied. "I suppose there's a lot to be said for. . . immediacy."

He smiled. "That's right! It's that golden resource known as *living memory*."

§

37

As I drove Linda home at the end of that first day at Eric's, I tried to get her to give me some idea of how much was left to be done. She was reluctant to give a definite answer - she didn't seem to want to think about it. "Well," I persisted, "do you think it will be finished tomorrow?"

"Probably not."

"So, it'll need a third day." She didn't answer. I patted her on the shoulder and said, "Whatever it takes." She turned to give me a fleeting smile that made me feel good, that I had said the right thing.

When we got home, Linda said she was too tired to go out or to do anything much that evening and so, after we had eaten, we sat down to watch TV. We soon found there was nothing either of us wanted on any channel and we decided to listen to music instead.

Like me, Linda still had an old style 'music centre' with turntable, cassette and CD players. I asked if she had an MP3 player. No, she said; and neither had I. It was another of those things, like sat nav, that I might get around to one day.

We reached an impasse when deciding what to play. It struck me as odd that, having known each other for so long, albeit with a 50 year gap, we knew nothing of each other's appetite or preferences in music. We talked about it and about John's tastes because many of the discs and cassettes on the shelves had been his. We seemed to like a lot of the same classical stuff, ranging through J.S. Bach, Mozart and Beethoven to Vaughan Williams. They liked Mahler; I liked Mendelssohn. I put on a CD of Vaughan Williams but, though we said how much we appreciated the beauty of the first track, we agreed it just wasn't right for us at the moment! Half an hour of trial and error later, having tried various 60s and 70s things, we settled for Ella Fitzgerald and Nat King Cole and other easy listening. Then we went back to TV to catch the news and weather before calling it a night.

We were up early next morning and on the road by 8.30.
Linda was in a good mood. "It is just possible I can finish today," she said. "You will keep out of our way, won't you? Be a good boy and don't distract Eric by getting him into discussions."

"All right - well, not until you've finished working."

We talked about our children during the rest of the journey. Linda revealed that her daughter, Sarah, had expressed interest in meeting me. To my surprise and encouragement she went on to speculate about when this might take place.

On arriving, they went straight to work. I settled down at the kitchen table with the books I had brought - a mystery novel and a book that Eric had lent me on memory research. His talk of 'living memory' and its importance to his work had ignited my interest in questions of memory and forgetting. My promise to Linda not withstanding, I found myself looking forward to getting an opportunity to talk to him about it.

Throughout the day I kept my promise and restricted myself to minimal exchanges with Eric. This was difficult over lunch because he seemed eager to take a break and to talk at length. Linda wasn't in the least inclined to join in any chatter so I stepped in for the sake of politeness but kept my restraint.

They stopped work at about 5.00. There was still some finishing off to be done, meaning we had to go in the next day, but it shouldn't take more than the morning, Eric declared with confidence, adding, "As soon as it's finished I'll take you both out for a pub lunch."

I could talk to him now the work was done and I was released from my promise. I began by asking him if he knew of ways of improving memory. Disappointingly, he seemed to have little interest in this practical, real life matter. He mentioned things I already knew about, including methods which, he explained, went back to the Ancient Greeks, such as placing things in rooms within a mental image of a familiar building; and he talked about using visual cues and other tricks. I listened patiently, not being interested so much in better methods of memorising data - I wanted to hear about ways of off-setting the deterioration that comes with age - but he had nothing to say about this. I realised he was trying to make a point and get me to change the way I thought about 'memorising': his preferred word.

His voice began to take on a lecturing tone. I didn't mind, but I felt a bit awkward when I caught sight of the expression on Linda's face.

"Let's take a look," he said, "at the three stages or processes supposed to be involved: recording, retention and retrieval. We have always had plenty of metaphors. We're particularly spoilt for metaphors for the recording stage - writing, wax tablets, photography, magnetic tape, putting things into boxes. And, what happens in the tape or the boxes? Well, the contents can persist, or fade, or they can decay, or become tangled and interfere with each other. And, as we know from our problems as we get older, the more things in the boxes the harder it is to find what we want. Metaphors galore!

"But we're too prone to thinking of the third stage, retrieval, as simply re-examining things, looking at them again, or taking them out of the box and putting them back. But that's too simplistic. It's only recently - relatively speaking - that we've begun to look at retrieval differently. There had previously been a sort of blind spot when it comes to the business of retrieval. Starting with. . ."

"Please," interrupted Linda, softly but forcefully, "could you continue this tomorrow. I want to go home!"

38

We arrived very early the next morning. It occurred to me that Eric might not be up yet, but he'd already completed his customary morning walk and was ready to start work.

Trying to settle in my usual place in the kitchen, I found I was feeling too fidgety to be able to concentrate on reading so I decided to followed Eric's example and go for a walk. I went out the front door and set off along the road I had taken back in June, trying to find my abandoned car. I recalled the sense of relief, of elation, that I'd felt that day. We had survived; and, as long as the car was OK, we were going home.

As I walked I scanned the ditches and hedge banks at the side of the road, naming the seasonal flowers as they came into sight: Meadowsweet, Agrimony. . . The once churned and muddy places by field gate entrances were now bright with fresh grass and luminous buttercups. I came upon a plant I didn't recognise and, while studying it, I suddenly remembered a recent dream. I was with Margaret, walking beneath trees and seeing unfamiliar plants and asking her their names. She was replying, but I couldn't make out what she was saying. The setting, the trees and the flowers were very strange, bizarre; and yet the dream held a sense of homely familiarity and joy.

On the way back, approaching the house, I caught sight of the scaffolding up against the once endangered wall. There was no sign of anyone working there, and I wondered how long it was going to take.

It was just after 10.00 when I arrived. I looked into the study to find them fully engrossed - the only sound being the faint clickety-click of two keyboards. I asked if they wanted coffee and then glanced at the papers spread out on Linda's table. "Still transcribing the old notes?" I asked, unnecessarily. She nodded and gave me a fleeting smile. I left the room feeling apprehensive that the work would not come to an end that morning after all, perhaps not even that day.

I was startled from my book by Linda flinging open the kitchen door and declaring, "Finished!" She looked relieved, but not particularly jubilant.

I stood up, stretched, and went across to her. "At last!" was all I could think of saying.

Eric appeared behind her, smiling, and said, "Ready to go for lunch? If you'll leave by the front door I'll bring the car round."

"No need - we'll go in my car," I said. Being aware that I couldn't drink, having to drive back to Linda's, I thought I'd give them the chance of celebrating.

Half an hour later we were sitting in warm shade in the pub garden, deciding what to have to eat. I tried to extend my magnanimity by offering to buy them Champagne but they both declined graciously. Eric pointed out that he would be working after we had departed; and anyway, this was the end of his long working relationship with Linda, not something to be celebrated. He then said, "I'm very grateful to you as well, Mike. When the work is completed and the last part published - if I'm still alive - I want you both to come to my celebration." He grinned. "It won't exactly be a commercial book launch."

We turned to the business of choosing what to eat. "I can recommend the fish, chips and peas," said Eric. "I don't know what their secret is with the fish but it's quite superior here." We both took his advice.

At some point Eric and Linda started to exchange anecdotes about their time in the world of academe. I was soon hearing all sorts of things about John's professional life -

things that Linda might never have mentioned to me, had she not been talking to Eric.

I forget exactly what prompted it. Eric had begun to talk specifically about some of the research he'd been carrying out before retiring; and I saw a chance of asking a question I'd been postponing, having promised Linda to behave myself.

"It's to do with forgetting. Sorry Linda, but this is the only chance I'll get - we'll be going home soon. Eric, every now and then you come across the notion that nothing is actually lost in memory. It's all there - the problem is retrieving it. What I want to know is: are there ways of improving the retrieval of old memories?"

Eric frowned. "You're not talking about so-called recovered memories, are you?"

"No - not in the sense of recovering memories of trauma and abuse. I was just wondering if there might be ways of enriching our ordinary memory for the past."

"Well, there are ways of improving recall of that kind," he said. "One is to try to reinstate the setting in which the experience, the learning took place." He expanded on this, but lost my interest when he began to talk about eyewitness testimony and the police.

I interrupted, "Aren't there any general. . . more powerful ways?"

"What sort of thing did you have in mind?"

I wasn't sure, but I asked, "What about these cognitive enhancement drugs?"

He shrugged dismissively. "I've never heard of any that can do what you want." He paused and then looked at me pointedly as he said, "You know, you shouldn't make the assumption that everything experienced is memorised. This is where we need to talk of *learning* - to recall something it has to have been recorded in the first place."

I was taken aback by this - I hadn't thought of this sort of memory in terms of learning. Then I remembered something.

"But isn't everything we experience remembered to some extent? I remember reading somewhere of an analogy. Think of the smooth surface of a swimming pool, at the start of a day. Then people start to dive and jump and swim in it. Every action performed in that pool leaves a lasting memory in the patterns of waves and reflections."

He smiled and put on a pained, resigned look. "Ah, these seductive metaphors!"

I felt a bit annoyed at this response. "I was only asking about a general principle. I wondered whether, because everything has memory, in a sense, then. . ."

Eric was smiling sceptically again. "I have come across speculation along those lines - the idea that everything has memory." He shrugged and looked to one side. I waited, careful not to glance in Linda's direction. Eventually he said, "Let's get back to human beings. . . and animals. I think your question was 'Isn't everything we experience remembered to some extent?' and I would reply: not in any meaningful sense. Some experiences, usually linked to an emotional response, leave lasting pictorial images. There are flashbulb memories, as they are called. People remember exactly where they were and what they were doing when they heard the news of some big event. In my days the example was hearing of the assassination of President Kennedy. But when it comes to the mass of unimportant experiences that you're referring to, I would guess that any information, in whatever sense, that they contain would attenuate and vanish in the background of noise. It would not be practically retrievable. It might not even be theoretically retrievable.

"Oh well," I replied, having seen what he was driving at, "it was just a thought!"

Linda joined in the conversation at that point and we talked of similar flashbulb memories for big public events in our own lives. They were fairly obvious ones - the deaths of John Lennon and Diana; Margaret Thatcher quitting; 9/11.

Eric suddenly declared that it was time to go. On the way back to his house he talked about the situation regarding the remaining work. It sounded as though there was still a lot to be done before Volume Three could be put to bed. He then spoke of his impatience to get back to the final volume and talked again about the value of living memory - of recording the things he knew of first hand. He gave us a list of the research areas and issues to be covered in writing about the late Twentieth Century.

Linda suddenly asked about consciousness and whether he would be dealing with it in Volume Four. I was intrigued by this and picked up a lot from the ensuing talk. It seemed that this was an area he had largely avoided, even though covering what he called 'levels of awareness' and their 'neurological correlates' including brain scans.

It dawned on me, as I listened to what Linda said, that her interest in the matter was very much *sui generis*, nothing to do with working with Eric.

§

39

We drove most of the way back to Linda's place in silence. On arriving we sat in the car, not moving, as if we didn't know what to do next.

I asked, "How are you feeling, now it's over?"

"A bit flat," she said. "Bleak."

"Is it like you feel when your exams have all finished? You've been yearning for that time to come but when it does you felt empty."

She turned to look at me. "I don't know. You've taken more exams in your life than I have."

After we had taken our things indoors and sat down to two large mugs of tea, we seemed to slump once more.

Then I said, "Let me take you out for a really nice meal tonight. We should celebrate. Mind you, we ought to go easy after the luxury of our celebratory lunch with Eric."

"I don't like you being sarcastic. But thank you for your offer - that sounds good."

Some time around eight that evening we were in a restaurant in Shrewsbury, consuming a bottle of good wine and a selection of *tapas* style dishes.

I had thought that our mood would be blithe and elated by this time but it wasn't even light. I looked at Linda. She wasn't looking so tired any more; and she seemed to be enjoying the food. But even though she was quite willing to talk about this and that, she wasn't very animated.

At some point Eric was mentioned. I went on to say how I would miss being able to talk with him. "About all sorts of things - to do with science history, not just psychology." She didn't reply and I remarked, "You were talking to him about consciousness, weren't you?"

"I tried," she said with a little smile. "It's a subject that interests me, but one that he doesn't like. He thinks it's beyond the remit of proper scientific psychology. He calls it a 'tumbling ground for whimsies'. That's a quote from William James - referring to notions of the *un*conscious mind."

"Oh well, at least you won't have to hear me going on about memory any more. I'm well aware it's not a topic that interests you."

"You're wrong," she said. "It *does* interest me. What I don't like is the way you go on about it. You're not just interested - with you it sounds obsessive. Your tone of voice changes when you talk about it. You're a different person - quite different from the Mike who talks enthusiastically about plants and nature. That's the nice Mike - the one who's kind, and amusing and. . . agreeable."

I forget the words I used in my reply - I was experiencing that hot, hurt feeling of being reproached.

She continued, "When you go on bemoaning your lack of photos and video and sound records, it's as if you won't accept ordinary forgetting. It's like you're desperately trying to claw back the past, isn't it?"

I thought about it. "You're right," I heard myself saying. During the next minute or so during which neither of us spoke I had a bit of insight. "It's something I got into after Maggie died," I said. "It's partly to do with feeling guilty. I didn't appreciate her. Well, no, that's not right - I *did* appreciate her, very much, but in lots of ways I took her for granted. I took life for granted. I keep telling myself I should have been more aware, and more grateful, during all those years . . . the happy years when the children were young." Something else came to mind. "And I didn't grieve properly. I kept on trying to escape - in stupid, unhelpful ways."

"You're not the only one to do that," she said. "I've been there too, remember. After John died I didn't grieve calmly - I was quite deranged for a time. All kinds of bad feelings and wrong thinking."

Here was something else I'd been giving no thought to. "I didn't realise," I said. "You've never talked to me about that."

"It's not been easy to talk to you in that way. You're not an encouraging person in that respect."

It was painfully obvious what she meant: always too busy talking about my own concerns. "I'm sorry," was all I could say.

We talked about our bereavement, and the stupid things we had both done in the years that followed. We laughed as we described the unlikely people we had briefly got involved with in our attempts to escape misery and loneliness. We also remembered and recounted how much we appreciated the kindness that others had shown us.

This change of mood, so unexpected, so positive, stayed with us through the rest of the meal and the taxi ride home.

We sat in armchairs half facing each other, just as we had during that first evening together at Linda's, in the winter. I commented on this and on remembering such little, sentimental things in life. Then I spoiled the moment by saying, "Of course, you don't like talking about memories."

"I don't mind exchanging memories - or even discussing them in an ordinary, non-obsessive way. I told you."

"Are you sure?"

"I'm sure. And that reminds me of something I wanted to say to you before." She reached across to hold my hand. "I never thought you would get much satisfaction from talking to Eric on the subject. As you know, his background is hard-nosed experimental psychology. He's not inclined to address the matter in the way you want."

Feeling a bit puzzled, and cautious, I asked, "What way is that? I'm not sure what you're getting at."

"Autobiographical memory - it's close to all our hearts, isn't it. But Eric is not interested, professionally. It's my impression, for what it's worth, that he's neglected it. . . along with social psychology aspects and. . . it's difficult to explain at this time of night." She stood up and stretched in a very attractive, feminine way.

"Come and sit on my lap while you're telling me," I suggested.

She did so; and then said, "Emotions have a lot to do with how much we remember from different times in our lives. . ."

"Oh yes," I said. "I've been reading about that. Emotional arousal having both positive and negative effects on later recall. . ."

"Don't interrupt!" she said, giving me a gentle smack on the back of my hand. "I'm not talking about experiments - Eric's kind of thing. What I'm referring to is different - something he would probably label as 'folk psychology' and be very dismissive about. . . But that's enough for now - let's leave all this unimportant stuff for another time." She gave me a perfunctory kiss to shut me up.

§

40

Our holiday was arranged, at last. The day after I got home I had an email from Linda to say that she had been on the internet and had found just the kind of thing we had in mind: a cottage for a week, self-catering. "In the Forest of Dean, half way between us." I only had to reply, to agree, and she would arrange it. I replied by calling her on the phone, being impatient to know where it was so that I could find it on the map.

She told me, and went on to say, "Unfortunately, it's a bit basic. We have to provide our own bed linen and towels. You'll have to bring them in your car. I'm going by train and I can only carry so much luggage."

I agreed to everything and left her to book it. Then I thought more about the matter of luggage and called her back. "Let me come and collect you," I said. "I know we ought to use public transport but you'll be limited in what you can bring." She wouldn't hear of it.

I met her at the railway station in Lydney. The first thing we did was to go shopping for the list of food and other items we had negotiated. Then we set out to find the place.

We soon found that the map I'd downloaded wasn't much help and we twice had to ask the way. "Isn't it time you got a sat-nav?" taunted Linda.

The plain smooth wall, up against the road, was either cob or rendered stone. Its colour, pink, had helped us find it, but it looked wrong to me - it belonged in East Anglia - cottages in the west are mostly white. It was empty of features apart from two little windows peeping out from beneath the gutter and a wooden plaque bearing its name. The front door was round to the left half-hidden by the over-grown shrubs of a tiny garden and parking area. We found the key, as instructed, under one of the white stones that flanked the path to the door.

We decided to make an exception of the first evening by eating out. While Linda was changing I went for a quick look around the outside. A flagstone path from the front door led round to a narrow back garden, the length of the house, separated from the woods beyond by a low, neatly clipped hedge. Half way along was a small concrete patio, complete with rotary clothes drier, and the back door. I couldn't continue further round the house because the ground at the other end was blocked off by a fence behind which was a mass of overgrown shrubs and trees. I guessed it belonged to the next house, about thirty yards down the road.

During the pub meal we were both feeling quite exuberant and we reminisced about childhood holidays - hers with relations in Radnorshire, mine in boarding houses on the Kent coast. When we got back to the cottage we noticed how light it still was and agreed to have a short drive and a walk to explore our surroundings before turning in.

Minutes later we stopped to walk among huge, monumental trees, bronze and golden where caught by the setting sun.

"I've been noticing oak and ash," said Linda, "but I don't recognise these."

"Sweet chestnut," I was able to say. "They're amazing, aren't they, when they've grown to this size."

We continued walking in silence. I noticed her shoes - they didn't look suitable for woodland walking. She guessed what I was thinking and said, "You needn't worry, I've brought some proper boots. I couldn't be bothered to unpack." This led to me mentioning my concern about her luggage restriction. "Don't worry! I've brought the essentials," she said; "and I managed to find room for my sketching things and my note-book. And a novel - something I've been looking forward to reading."

"I've brought a couple of books," I said. She squeezed my hand. "Were you going to say something?" I asked.

There was enough light for me to see her give one of her mischievous smiles. "I was thinking of us, fifty years ago. We wouldn't have bothered bringing anything to read, would we?"

Back at the cottage once more, I was pleasantly surprised when I entered the sitting room for the first time. Jutting into the room at one end was a lumpy, rustic stone chimney breast. Beneath a huge lintel, the firebox was flanked on each side by deep, high spaces filled with stacked logs. "This is cosy," I said. "What is it they call fireplaces like that?"

"Estate agents call them inglenooks, but I understood that a real inglenook is supposed to be big enough to sit in. I don't think you could manage that in this one."

"Well," I said, "the whole room is a pleasant surprise. I've just had a thought: this would be a nice place to spend Christmas."

"And I've just realised," she said, "that this is your first glimpse of it. When we arrived I set off to explore the rooms while you wanted to scrutinize the outside."

"We're so different, aren't we?" I responded. "Do you think there's any hope for us?"

§

41

Next morning, after breakfast, we were sitting outside on the concrete patio, looking across to woodland and pale blue sky in the west. Linda was making a watercolour sketch of two nearby trees with a glimpse of distance between them. Watching her work, I recalled her saying how she had brought 'my sketching things and my note-book'. I asked, "You said you'd brought a note-book with you - was that for making notes on me and the state of our relationship?"

She grinned and carried on working. Then she said, "I always take a note-book with me. Bright ideas pop into your head and then get forgotten."

"What sort of ideas?"

"For something I'm writing."

I was about to bombard her with eager questions but, just in time, I remembered an event from the past and stopped. Soon after we married I had been surprised to discover that Maggie had been secretly writing things - poetry mainly. My questioning had become nothing short of boorish. She had stopped me by saying, good-naturedly, "Tread softly, for you tread upon my dreams." I discovered later that this was a misquote although I liked the rhythm of her version as much as that of Yeats himself.

"Oh. . ." I said to Linda eventually. "Are you going to tell me about it?"

"I might - but not just now." She continued to paint in silence.

A little later, feeling restless and not in the mood to read, I said, "I'm going for a walk - just a short one. Do you want to join me?"

"Later, maybe. I'd like to finish this while the light is so good."

I set off, soon leaving the road to climb a grassy slope and begin exploring the ground beneath the smooth trunks of trees so tall I couldn't make out what kind they were. I was on the lookout for two things: tracks or any other signs of the wild boar that I had heard about; and any fungi that I could identify confidently as edible and bring back for cooking.

For half an hour or so I didn't see a single human being and I began romancing to myself about the remoteness and wildness of this forest that I'd never got round to visiting before. Linda's mention of writing had sparked a memory of my early days of writing science fiction and fantasy; and this dark wood was just the place to inspire ideas. Then I saw a man approaching, wearing a green Barbour coat and wellington boots. After exchanging good mornings I asked about the wild boar: is this a likely part of the forest; and what signs do I look for? He answered, "Possibly." He then described the churned up ground and the exact shape of the hoof prints. Soon after we parted I decided it was time to turn back. Then I realised I had lost my way.

It didn't take long for me to work out that if I kept going downhill I should at least find my way back to the road. Once I found it I would have to look for landmarks indicating whether I needed to go left or right.

On reaching the road I could see nothing I recognised so I had to guess. I was either intuitive or just lucky because I eventually came within sight of two houses, one of them the unmistakable pink. Slightly puzzled by the juxtaposition of the two buildings I stopped to get a better idea of the lie of the land. I took out my binoculars and looked at our cottage. From that position I could see into the back garden and the patio. There was Linda, still painting. It was strange, interesting, to see her like this. I had always seen her close up, never from a distance - not counting that 'magpie' signal from the window of Eric's house - and never when she was unaware of being seen. As I looked at her I felt a sudden uprush of tenderness and yearning - I just couldn't wait to get back, to be with her.

Linda seemed quite taken aback and even a bit amused at the way I kissed her as soon as I arrived. I eventually let her go and turned to go into the house. Then I remembered something: when walking down to the road on the way back I had come upon some edible Boletus mushrooms, reasonably maggot-free and worth gathering. I took them out of my shoulder bag and presented them to her.

"What am I supposed to do with those?"

"Well, you needn't do anything. If you remember, it's my turn to cook lunch today. I'd already decided to make an omelette, so now we can have mushroom omelette."

"Could you make two lots - one with fungus and one without?"

"If you insist. Don't you trust my judgement?"

She didn't reply but, as I went to go into the kitchen, she said, "You will put some aside, won't you. You'll need a sample to take with you in the ambulance."

I laughed as I visualised the scenario: me clutching my abdomen and rolling on the floor; Linda phoning for the ambulance. That made me check my mobile - no signal. I got her to check hers - likewise. We were indeed isolated. But I still ate and enjoyed my mushroom omelette.

After lunch, it was Linda who was keen to go for a walk. It had begun to rain about midday but we found that the trees afforded some protection and we were able to ignore it for a while. However, the weather was having a dampening effect on our mood and after half an hour we turned round to go back.

"How are you feeling?" she asked. "Any belly-ache, nausea, dizziness?"

"No. You needn't worry - I'm very familiar with some of the edible kinds. I've been eating them for years."

"You've got me looking out for toadstools myself," she said, "but I haven't seen any yet."

"Well, it's a bit early in the year - you don't see many until the autumn. If I spot one of interest I'll let you know."

It was through 'having my eye in' in this way that I did notice something of interest and I stopped to photograph it.

"That's the first time since we've been here that I've seen you use your camera," she said.

"Well," I replied, "I've changed my behaviour. Things you've been saying to me have made me think." I was about to tell her of some recent discernments of mine but I thought it better to leave it till later.

§

42

The rest of the afternoon was wet and rather dark but this created the right mood for the 'evening of indulgence' we had planned. We drove into Lydney to buy vegetables and other food items. Linda did most of the choosing. As I get older I find it hard to plan or even think rationally about food unless I'm hungry; and if I'm very hungry I go to the other extreme and impulse buy. She mentioned the tapas we'd had in Shrewsbury and suggested a meal along the same lines. It sounded unnecessarily elaborate to me but I agreed and even contributed an idea or two.

It was fun preparing the food in spite of the poorly equipped and unfamiliar kitchen and I enjoyed helping to overcome the different problems that arose. Small quantities of savoury dishes, not too herby or spicy, to be accompanied by Spanish red wine. Linda pointed out that the dishes weren't really very Spanish so I invented the word 'tapoid' to describe the meal.

It was a great success and there was nothing left over. After I had persuaded Linda to let me leave the washing up until the morning we got up and went to sit on the sofa at the other end of the room.

One of us switched on the little TV, purely out of habit because we paid no attention to it, both of us lapsing into gratified silence. It then crossed my mind to take a photo or two to preserve that moment of contentment. I stood up to get my camera, and then remarked regretfully that I should also have taken pictures of that lovely food spread out on the table before we started.

"Don't be such a spoiler!" she scolded. "I thought you were getting over your compulsion." I went back to the sofa and cuddled up to her.

An hour or so later, after watching the 10.00pm news, we switched off the TV and sat silent for a while. Then Linda said, "Dawn was talking to me the other day, about photographs. She inherited a load of them when her brother died. They were stowed away in a box and she wondered whether they'd ever been looked at since being put there. We talked about photos and mementoes - your influence - and wondered about the millions of digital images that are going to be passed on to future generations everywhere.

"Well," I replied, "our kids will have them as an archive should they want to. . . make use of them."

"But it goes beyond just photos and video, doesn't it. Dawn was telling me how someone she knows is preserving all his emails, all his social networking stuff. And that reminded me of something I've read about called life-logging. Apparently, there are people who have begun to record every moment of their own and their children's lives. We wondered how anyone would find the time to look at all that. . .stuff. Will people just give up living the present, for the sake of reliving the past - in real time? Or will it just be put aside and passed on to the future?"

"Well," I said, "the answer would lie in properly editing all our stuff."

"I don't want to get you started again but it's just another metaphor for the way we make our autobiographical memory, isn't it?"

"All right," I said, "I promise I won't go down that road!"

Minutes later I broke that promise. Linda was speaking about this having been a gratifying start to our holiday. I agreed, referring to some of the small pleasures of the day. Then I began to muse wistfully about how little would be left in future memory. She said nothing and I went further: "I have these great gaps for periods in my life. Don't misunderstand me - I'm not talking about amnesia. I had a bit of that once, after falling and knocking myself out, but it was only for the previous hour or so, and it all came back eventually, except for the last few seconds before the fall. No, I mean chunks of my life that seem to have left almost no memories."

"I'm guessing," she interrupted, "that these were happy and contented times."

"That's right - I was just going to say that!"

"Well, goodness me, it's not just you - other people find the same thing. Soon after I married John we got our first decent flat - a nice big one. That was a really happy time, and yet I only have a few clear memories of it. There was one room in the place that I know was there, but I remember nothing about it whatever - as if I'd never been in it. A year or so later, when we moved into our first house - rented, of course - it was different. That was the time of my pregnancy and Heulwen being born and it's full of picture memories as well as music - the very first Beatles songs. It depends what's happening in your life, doesn't it."

"I suppose so. Some special times have left their memories. But what seems wrong," I almost said 'unfair', "is that the clearest, most detailed recollections are of times when. . ." I stopped. So far, since getting to know her again, I had avoided telling her about all that.

"When bad things happened? Like tragedy? Loss?"

"Yes! But nothing so justifying as tragedy and loss. I'm talking about. . . when I was in a depression."

She paused before asking, very quietly, "Why do you feel unjustified and guilty about depression?"

I shrugged. "I just do."

She waited for me to say more. I didn't. She continued: "It's just a fact of life. The memories that last are the ones that are full of emotional experiences. You must have *some* lasting memories of the special, happy times."

"Yes, of course - exciting times when I was a child - such as Christmases." I stopped because I had just recalled something really pertinent. "I used to have a wonderful, timeless, extended memory of being with *you*! It was one afternoon soon after we met. A bright spring afternoon that went on forever. We were strolling about in that little dingle on the edge of town."

"Why did you say you *used* to have this memory?"

"Well, in later times, after we'd parted, I often recalled that moment - dwelling on it, treasuring it but, even though I say I remember it now, I'm only remembering the *memory*. The moment and its magic have gone."

She cuddled up to me. I was suddenly aware of what I had been doing but I didn't speak then, not wanting to spoil the moment. Eventually I said, "I've broken my promise and gone on about memory."

"It's all right," she said, very quietly. "Look, I haven't said much before because of the way you've been - a bit boring, and overwhelming, isn't it - but I do have an interest in the subject. That writing I mentioned - well it's important there. No, not now! I'll tell you about it later."

§

43

The weather looked promising the next morning and we were keen to make the most of it and do some exploring. Knowing nothing of the Forest we thought we'd do the conventional thing and start by visiting the museum and heritage centre, north east of our cottage.

We set out about 10.00 with Linda navigating. While studying the map, she noticed the place name 'Symonds Yat' and exclaimed, "I've been there! I was taken there as a child." She described being lifted up to look down into the Wye Gorge and being terrified as well as thrilled at her first glimpse of its tumbling green walls. "I'd like to see it again - can we go there today?" So we changed our plans and headed north west - we'd go to the heritage centre some other time.

Our journey took us through Coleford where we stopped briefly and bought a guidebook on Dean Forest walks. Eventually, we ended up, by an indirect route, on the north side of the River Wye.

From the car park we embarked on a long straight trek, following a lane and then muddy and rocky tracks. On our right was a landscape of broad-leaf and conifer woodland - 'Lord's Wood', the book informed us. The midday sun shone from that direction, sometimes through trees, when it diminished their colours, but sometimes upon them where it warmed them to brighter yellows and greens. We talked about the colours, recalling the varied hues of the spring foliage when we were staying with Dennis and Gwen and contrasting it with the bland, dark green vista that broad-leaf trees can present at this time of year, unless the sun is shining upon them, as now.

Autumn wasn't far away; and this awareness prompted us to discuss what we might be doing later in the year. Both of us seemed to be avoiding the matter of whether we would still be 'an item' by then; and we restricted out talk to such things as Linda's holiday with Hayley, next month, and my vaguely planned visit to - or from: we hadn't decided - Felicity and family.

We were distracted from this when, on our way down to the river, we passed some caves - which I resisted the temptation to investigate - and a quarry, similarly resisted, until we came into Symonds Yat West.

I resisted because we were hurrying. We had both remarked on how hungry we were; and the book had informed us that when we reached the river we could cross it by ferry to reach a pub - 'The Saracen's Head'. An exciting and motivating prospect.

Sitting outside the pub, sipping coffee after our meal, we remained silent for a long time, enjoying without comment the sweep of the river and the green and rocky splendour of the opposite bank. I began to regret not having done some pre-holiday homework on the geology of the area.

Linda was the first to speak. She described a book by an author she knew who was enamoured of the Wye Valley and its towns and history.

Choosing my words and tone with care I asked, "Is this a good time to ask about *your* writing?"

"All right, but don't expect me to talk about it in detail." Long pause. "It's a novel."

"Oh. Can I ask what sort? Is it a romance, a crime novel?"

"Neither - it isn't a genre novel. And I'm surprised at your suggesting I'd want to write crime fiction. It's about a family and its history. I suppose it could be called a saga."

"Not an Aga saga, I trust?"

She gave me a pained look. "I hope not."

"Anyway, you haven't got an Aga. Your stove is a Rayburn, like mine."

She said nothing at first and I regretted my silly comment. But then she smiled and said, "How about a 'Rayburn *roman*'?"

"Very good!"

After another pause, during which I almost gave up hope of hearing any more, she continued, "It's something I started years ago and then put to one side. I thought of it recently and went up into the loft to search for the manuscript. A loft is another metaphor for a memory store, isn't it?"

"So it is," I replied, "and so is a cellar."

"That sounded so gloomy!" I shrugged. She continued, "After reading it through - paper copy, of course, done on my old electric typewriter - I tried to see why it had ground to a halt in its original form. Then I suddenly thought of a much better way of. . . constructing it. *You* can take some credit for that because. . ."

Even though I was aware of a forth-coming compliment, I interrupted her, eager to know, "Is it your first novel?"

"No. I completed another one, a long time ago. And I've made starts on two - no, three - others, but they came to nothing."

"Oh. . ." I was so taken aback by this hitherto unknown part of her life that, even though I wanted to hear more, I was lost for words.

"Shall we go now," she said. "We ought to get back across the river while we can and get on with our walk."

We returned uphill, along the road that had taken us to the riverside and soon got back to the path mapped out in red in the guidebook. The rest of the walk - the main part - would take us south, then west, then north as it followed the big horseshoe sweep of the river, around the other side of the wood and to various features of interest.

But it was not to be. As soon as we rejoined the walk, Linda said, "Would you mind very much if we didn't go the rest of the way. My leg has been hurting. I didn't say anything before because I hoped it might just be stiffness and would get better. But it hasn't. I don't think I could make it all that way. I hope I can make it back to the car." I must have shown my disappointment because she chided me: "You don't want to have to carry me!"

So we made the most of a leisurely stroll back the way we had come. We walked hand in hand and talked about all sorts of things that I don't now remember.

§

44

The sky clouded over during the night and we got up next morning to find it raining steadily, drearily.

"How is your leg this morning?" I asked, over breakfast.

"A bit stiff but no problem."

"What would you like to do today?" Linda just looked thoughtful so I went on, "Shall we go to the information centre, and then take it from there?" We'd finished eating so I stood up and began to gather the plates and things.

"Would you mind if we left that to the afternoon?" she replied. "I'd like just to sit indoors this morning. . . maybe do a bit of writing. Now that I've resurrected that novel I keep getting new ideas."

"You should have brought a lap-top with you."

"No need - with me it's hand-written first. Anyway, I want to work on revising the whole thing and that's going to mean lots of little notes."

My first response had been to feel a bit peeved - she was going to cut herself off, do her own thing, while I was going to be at a loose end, without any motivation as yet for doing anything on my own. But now my curiosity sparked into life.

"It sounds like one huge project," I said; "and you want to embark on it today? - in the middle of our short, get-to-know-each-other-better, holiday?"

She stood up and came round the table to give me a hug and a peck on the cheek. "I'm sorry," she said. "Just let me have the morning."

That made a difference. "You have as long as you like," I said, kissing her. "I think I'll go for a walk even though it is raining. I might find some more fungi to poison you with."

She smiled and said, "It's your fault - I told you, didn't I, that you can take credit for inspiring this new beginning."

"It's nice to know I've been of some use. Do you want to tell me in what way?"

"It's to do with memory. But no more discussion just now - let me make a start while I'm still bubbling. I'll tell you more later."

By the time I was ready to set out the rain had stopped, so I thought I might take the car and go a bit further for my excursion. I had been map browsing that morning, looking for places to visit; and I'd noticed various lakes, chains of ponds and other prospects of interesting water that I felt drawn to explore. One such was Soudley Ponds, but that was next to the Dean Heritage Centre and we'd probably be going there later. Much nearer, and more suited to a short trip, was Mallards Pike Lake and I decided on that.

I thought of something: "Will it be all right if I go a bit further than before and take longer?"

"Of course," she replied.

"Don't forget, we can't contact each other - no mobile signal here."

"Don't worry about it."

Half an hour later, I was standing by a shapely expanse of water, looking at an information board. The place was a bit more tame and tidy than I'd anticipated when I saw it on the map. It occurred to me that it would make a pleasant, nonstrenuous walk to undertake with Linda. Should I leave it till later and go somewhere else today? No - that would keep me away longer. I started to amble round the edge of the lake, looking at the different kinds of vegetation on the margins. I took out my binoculars and began trying to identify various birds on the far side.

Big summer raindrops began to strike the still surface, making little pointed domes. I recalled that, as a child, I used to think they looked like fishing floats. There was a sharp call from a moorhen. And a watery smell. What was it? - fish slime?. . . water mint?. . that familiar pond scent of aerobic decay?

The questioning stopped.

Mike is standing by that lake in Essex. He is fishing, with his friends from primary school. Summer holidays.

The scene disappeared - I had become self-aware. Then it returned and I could see things in detail: the opposite bank of that other lake; reeds; bushy trees; the derelict old mansion we used to say was haunted. I tried to see the faces of my companions but that erased everything, leaving just a feeling of joy, of a simple kind I had forgotten.

I arrived back at the cottage about midday, feeling slightly anxious at having left Linda alone with no means of contact.

She was sitting, writing, at the little kitchen/dining table. She looked up and said, "Make us some coffee and I'll tell you about what I've been doing." After I had done so and we were sitting on the sofa, mugs in hand, she said, "I've written you a summary of what I'm trying to do - I did it for my own benefit as well as yours." She held a sheet of paper in her other hand and began to read from it. I could see across to what she'd written:

'Some members of a family, living in the present, are researching their ancestry. At the same time they are remembering their own pasts, and constructing their own personal histories, as they live their lives.

'What I'd already written began to feel a bit cut and dried, too certain. I now realise that I needed to allow for, and illustrate, the unreliability of memory - its capriciousness, its proneness to our unconscious agendas. The story will be more lively and enriched if I make more of the normal myth making and the confabulating that

goes on in their lives as they tell stories about themselves, each other and about events in the past.'

She put down her coffee mug and the paper and turned to me. "Well? Does that give you some idea?"

"Yes, it does - very impressive. What does confabulating mean?"

"Well, in psychology it means making things up to fill in memory gaps, and believing them."

"Do you mean like Jenny - your school friend?"

"Sort of. Jenny was worse - she used to fantasize - to the botheration of her friends."

"How long had you been working on the original version of this novel?"

"About two years, on and off."

"Well, it sounds as though it's going to take more years. I'm still feeling amazed - you've said nothing till now about your writing. Have you talked to anyone else about it?"

"My daughters. . . and some members of the book club. There's a group of three or four of us interested in writing; and every now and then they meet, and read bits to each other, and give helpful criticism."

"You said you'd completed another novel. Was that published?"

"No. I spent a lot of time and postage money trying, but no luck. One of the group - Sylvia - is a successful writer. She knows about the business side, and she's offered to help with getting agents and things like that."

"Will you let me read your other novel - you haven't destroyed it have you?"

"No, the manuscript is still gathering dust in the loft. I *might* let you read it."

By the time we arrived at the Dean Heritage Centre the thick soft grey of the sky had broken up into lumpy clouds on a ground of intense blue. We had some lunch at the centre before going to see the museum. After that we looked at the picturesque stone buildings on the rest of the site before setting out to walk around nearby Soudley Ponds.

"How's your leg?" I asked.

"OK at the moment. It got better as soon as we started walking; and I haven't felt any painful twinges so far."

"Whereabouts is the pain - is it your knee, your ankle?"

"It's the knee that's causing the problem, although the pain wanders about a bit. I had this trouble a year ago and I should have done something about it; but I kept putting it off and it got better."

There came a point where she had stopped to look at something and was now about twenty yards behind me. I watched her as she quickened her pace to catch up and could see no sign of the limp she had shown the previous day. I liked the way she walked - so familiar - I probably remembered it from the past, like her handwriting. Although she wore nothing remarkable - just her new walking boots, black jeans tucked into thick socks, light green shirt and dark green cotton jacket - she seemed sort of young and graceful.

As she caught up she reached out and took my hand; and we continued to amble along without talking, except to admire the occasional dragonfly that danced and darted along the water's edge.

§

45

Next morning it was Linda who raised the question as to what we would do that day. Her emphasis was on my wishes as opposed to ours and the reason soon emerged.

"I'm concerned about my leg," she said. "It's hurting again."

"Oh. . . that's a shame - you said yesterday's walk made it better?"

"It did, but as soon as I began walking about this morning I felt a twinge and it gave way - I nearly fell over. I'd rather stay here for the time being. It might get better during the day."

"Well, the weather looks good - we could sit in the garden. You could do some more painting, unless you think you've exhausted the possibilities of the view from here."

"Not likely," she said. "Cezanne painted the same view - a distant mountain - again and again."

"Is that what you'd like to do then?"

"Yes. . . or I might read."

"If you feel up to it we could go for a drive later. We could go to Monmouth or Chepstow - you wouldn't have to do much walking."

"I'm sorry if I've spoilt your day."

"Don't be daft," I replied. "I'll sit outside with you and read. Or we can just talk."

There was a fresh breeze but the air was warm enough for sitting outdoors in comfort. I started reading one of my books but soon I began to feel the need to move about, so I stood up and walked across to Linda to find her reading, not painting.

"Finished?"

"Waiting for part of it to dry."

I looked at the painting. There was something about it that reminded me of the scene at Mallards Pike and my experience there. I couldn't resist describing it to her, and I asked if she ever had any experiences like that.

"Yes - I expect many people do," she replied. She went on to mention Proust's madeleine moment.

"May I say something more about memory?" I asked.

"Go on then - if you must."

"I was going to say how remarkably accurate I've found some of my childhood memories can be. I'm talking mainly about visual memories. I've often found that if you see something you haven't seen since childhood it can look more or less exactly the same as you remembered it."

"I know what you mean," she said. "With me it's the books I had as a child - the ones with pictures. Sometimes I've come across a copy in a jumble sale, or a second-hand bookshop, and the pictures are just the way I remember them - after sixty years or more." She picked up a brush and began painting again.

"You didn't mind me indulging my obsession again, did you?"

"You don't sound obsessed any more. You've been much nicer lately."

I didn't know how to reply to that so I said nothing and just watched her work on her painting. I began to think more about life-long visual memories. Her example had reminded me of how some of my daughters' Ladybird books were ones I'd seen in my own childhood. Mainly the stories about animals such as kittens, mice and owls - the pictures were vividly the same as I remembered them.

Linda interrupted my reverie to say, "It occurs to me that we could be partly deceiving ourselves - doing a bit of confabulating. After all, it's only when we see the image again that we decide it matches our memory."

"Well, yes, but it can be so vivid - and unexpected."

"Even so, we could be adjusting things because we like them to match."

"I suppose you're right," I said. "It's *you* who should've been the scientist! If we could photograph the visual memories in our heads, before looking at the pictures again. . ."

"Only in your old science fiction."

She continued painting details into where the pale wash had dried. I stood up again and began to wander along the hedge, looking at the plants. When I got to the fence at the end I peered between the bushes and tree trunks that were pressed up against it and could see the ivy-covered back wall of the house next door; and a man standing by it, smoking. That would account for the smell of cigarette smoke I thought I'd noticed once or twice that morning. He saw me, waved and made his way across.

"Nice day," he said. A lean man in grubby jeans and a denim jacket and I recognised him as the Barbour-coated man I had spoken to earlier that week. He anticipated my next thought: "Any luck with the wild boar?"

"Not so far. Mind you, we haven't really been looking."

I learnt that he and his wife, who was inside the house, were owners of the place next door. It was another small holiday cottage, vacant at the moment, and they were there doing maintenance work and odd jobs. Their home was nearby - half a mile up the road. Linda came over to join us and shortly after that the man's wife appeared. The four of us continued talking until large drops of rain caused us to disperse.

The shower lasted hardly any time and, once Linda had made her painting safe, we decided to stay where we were and take a chance on the weather. Soon, the sky had cleared completely and we settled for enjoying the rest of the morning outside. The only interruption to our tranquillity was the harsh sound of our neighbour starting up a chain saw every now and then and using it to cut the boundary tree trunks -

the ones between which we had been having our conversation.

Early in the afternoon, after a snack lunch and lots of light conversation about nothing in particular, I said to Linda, "We don't have to go out if you don't want to. We don't need any shopping, do we?"

"Well, we could make do. Mind you, we've got nothing to drink - we're out of wine and beer."

"We've still got fruit juice and fizzy water, haven't we?"

"I can hardly believe I'm hearing that, from you," she said. "Come to think of it though, you have been drinking less the last couple of days."

We carried on just reading and talking every now and then. The noises from next door had changed: the snarl of the chain saw had been replaced by the rasp of a timber saw and the falling of leafy branches. All activity seemed to have come to an end by 4.00 and I strolled across to have a look at the changes. The grass on our side of the boundary was covered with leaves, branches and pieces of trunk. Not our problem, I reminded myself. Amongst the litter was a small log - a short length that had been cut at both ends. I picked it up and began to cast my eye over the annual growth rings on the cleanly cut surface; and then felt prompted to bring it across to show Linda. "Look," I said, "annual growth rings - each with a different thickness. That's something I find fascinating."

"Mm," she replied.

"That must have been a good summer," I said, pointing to a broad ring. "And that one next to it was probably a poorer one - colder maybe, or drier."

She looked up and said, "I can see why it's something you find interesting to think about. The tree carries a story of its past, like a diary, or a medical record, even."

"It's another metaphor for long-term memory!" I declared.

"That had crossed my mind too, but I avoided saying it. I didn't want to start you off."

"But. . ." Thoughts came tumbling into my mind faster than I could find the right words for. "It's. . . more than just a dead recording. . . the rings are alive. What I mean to say is, there is living tissue in the old rings. It's only when the trunk is older that the central heart-wood is alive no longer."

"So the rings are a kind of living history - a living memory?"

"Yes - wonderful, isn't it."

She put her book down and looked at me in a strange, intent way. "Don't you think you could take a lesson from this?"

"What do you mean?"

"Your big complaint - 'gripe' I should say - about memory, about not having kept much from your past life. Well, maybe you have. Just because you can't picture it or talk about it doesn't mean to say it doesn't exist. It may not be there as what's called 'declarative memory' - and you may think you've preserved nothing from those times, but in a sense you have." She put out her hand to hold my cheek, very lightly, and she smiled as she said, "You've absorbed the experiences, assimilated them. They've become a part of your *self*, the entire living organism that is Michael Rowe."

§

46

It was our last full day in the cottage and we were up early to make the most of it. Linda suggested we start by going for a short walk before breakfast to test her knee before making decisions about the rest of the day.

The sky, seen through the trees was a clear blue - a bright ceiling, supported by immensely tall pillars, blemished only by lingering vapour trails. The air was cold and full of reminders that September was only a week away. We talked of this as we walked, with our arms round each other, and tried to name the different scents.

We came to a clearing and stopped to be warmed up by the sun. There were brambles here, bearing a few ripe blackberries. We picked some and celebrated their being our first of the season. Slightly sour, but tasting of the coming autumn itself, distilled.

As we were clearing up after breakfast I asked, "How's the knee?"

"A lot better."

"It's a shame that it spoilt your holiday. I'll make it up to you, next time we go away." I waited in case she wanted to comment on that.

But all she said was, "If it starts being troublesome again I'm going to talk to my GP about getting it sorted. Being able to do serious walking is important to me. I've got plans."

"That sounds interesting. What have you got in mind?"

"Well, it sounds mad, me being in this state, but I hoped one day to walk Offa's Dyke - in easy stages, of course."

"That's something I'd like to do! We could. . ."

"So, I'm going to be cautious and take it easy today. No rough ground - I don't want to go twisting it, do I?"

"Oh. . . So what about our expedition to look for the wild boar?"

"I think you'd better do that on your own. Why don't you go now while it's still early?"

"What will you do?"

"A bit of writing. It should get warm enough to sit outside."

"All right then - I'll go now." I went to look for my camera and binoculars.

Just as I was about to leave she came across to give me a kiss and say, "Can you remember what Roy said?" Roy, the man from the cottage next door, had told us of a place where the beasts might be seen and had given detailed directions.

After half an hour or so of walking, mainly uphill, I found what could be the part of the Forest Roy had described. It was now a matter of keeping my eyes open. I'd been told to look out for a pit containing water - or it might be just mud, with the recent dry weather - which, he said, they used as a wallow when it was hot.

I came across such a pit, and it was filled with sticky mud. It didn't look too promising, being surrounded by human and dog footprints. What do I look for now? I wandered off to one side towards a large area of bracken.

And there, on a clear grassy patch in the middle, were the signs I'd been looking for - no mistake. Large chunks of turf and moss had been upturned and scattered, exposing black leaf mould. The ground looked as though it had been attacked by some out-of-control machine; or perhaps by giant hens - I'd seen what ordinary chickens can do to a lawn. But the prints I could just make out were not of bird talons but of hooves - cloven hooves.

My luck continued: while I was squatting on the ground examining the prints and manoeuvring myself to photograph them I heard a rustling sound coming from a few yards in front of me. I looked up. I can see it now, as if my first glimpse was a snapshot. We looked at each other - full face. A sinister smoky grey, high pointing ears and long, tapering snout. So tall, so unexpectedly vertical, quite unlike the round pig shape I must have been expecting. I swung my camera but it had gone, leaping like a hare into the bracken.

Satisfied that my quest had been fulfilled, I felt keen to get back to Linda. I set off, walking as quickly as I could, breaking into a run whenever I felt up to it, glad that it was mainly downhill.

By the time I came within sight of the cottage I was happy to slow down. My chest was hurting and I was feeling weak with exhaustion. As I drew nearer, something caught my attention: the fact that I couldn't see the car. I carried on at the same relaxed pace, thinking I must have parked it further back behind the bushes, or something like that. It was only when I got there that I realised it was actually missing.

I ran to the front door. It was locked. I called out, and grabbed the iron knocker and hammered hard, my heart itself beginning to hammer in my chest and head as puzzlement turned to alarm. No response. I ran round to the back. No Linda; and the back door was locked as well.

Standing there, trying to be rational and systematic, I questioned what had made me leap to the conclusion the car had been stolen. Could Linda have taken it? She was acutely reluctant to drive my car, never wanting to take a share on long journeys. But she may have had a good reason to go out in it. And, naturally, she would lock both doors.

There must be a note somewhere. I searched around the back, and then walked round to the front, ranting out loud about the lack of mobile phone signal. She must have left the note inside, and - of course - she would leave the key for me in the usual place.

It was there, under the white stone at the side of the path. I let myself in and began looking for the note in all the likely places - the sort where I would leave such a message. Nothing to be found - so, with growing anxiety and a sinking heart, I extended my search into unlikely places. Eventually I gave up and flopped in despair on the sofa.

At some point a hopeful idea took shape within the stew of helplessness: it was just possible that she'd left a message *with* the key. I recalled that I'd hurriedly grabbed the key from under the stone and I could have failed to notice it. I knew it was unlikely - a notion born of desperation - and I caught myself dawdling on the way out through the front door, as if to postpone the inevitable disappointment.

I counted my way along the stones by the path in reverse order, lifted up the right one, then - desperately, irrationally - the ones on either side. As I feared and knew, there was nothing there. But, on the whiteness, I noticed two bright circular spots of unmistakable colour - blood.

I must have launched into action without thought - just as I'd done the day I heard of Linda's plight in the floods - for the next thing I was aware of was going out of the gate, on to the road and running, making for the house next door.

The road curved round to meet the sun. I was blinded for a moment and had to halt while my eyes adjusted. Then, keeping my head down, I continued to walk until no longer in line with the rays.

There was a dark patch in the line of sight. I tried to see beyond it, assuming it to be an after-image, but as I moved my head it stayed where it was, fixed to the road. It was a human figure. Linda? I ran forwards, calling her name.

As I drew nearer it began to resolve to an individual form; and I could see that it was indeed like Linda. I called to her again in joyful recognition of that slight, trim, sweet shape that I knew so well - from fifty years before.

Reality penetrated and, as joy gave way to bewilderment, I heard a voice that was not Linda's, saying:

"Are you the man from next door? I've been looking out for you. Your wife has taken my dad to hospital."

That poor young woman - Tanya was her name. I couldn't wait to hear the explanation without firing questions at her. I finally got the story, in spite of my anxious interruptions. It seemed that Roy and his wife and daughter had been working in the back garden when whatever tool Roy was using had slipped and cut his arm, badly. The family had no car with them, having walked to the cottage that morning. Tanya and her mum had bandaged him up as best they could and had rushed him round to ask Linda to drive him to the A&E in Cinderford. There would obviously have been no time to leave a message.

After she had gone indoors, I went back to the cottage which now seemed sad and empty - a dreary little hovel. I still hadn't got over my feeling of queasy relief; and all I wanted to do was sit outside on the front doorstep, within sight of the road. Also in my sight was the blood-marked white stone that had been the only message.

I was startled when the car finally appeared in the road - it had not come from the direction I expected. I watched as Linda parked it carefully between the bushes, noticing she was alone.

"How's Roy?" I asked as soon as she emerged.

"He's all right. Discharged with a few stitches. I've taken him and Becky home."

I found myself saying, "No excuses from now on - you *can* drive my car!" Stupid remark - I'd wanted to say so much but didn't know how. Only when we were inside was I able to take her in my arms and say, "I thought I'd lost you." I could feel her bewilderment and so I explained about seeing the blood and not knowing what had happened until I heard from Tanya.

47

It was only later that night that I was able to express my newly recognised feelings and talk about the understanding that had been taking shape for me.

Neither of us had felt like doing anything in particular for what remained of that dramatic afternoon so, after a necessary trip to the nearest shops, we'd settled for some home cooking and an evening in.

Preparing the food together seemed an especially happy activity; I particularly remember chopping onions while we talked and joked. The first thing we spoke of was the business of going home the next day. I had been due to drop her off at the railway station in Lydney; but that now seemed a dismal thing to do - a sad anti-climax to our holiday - and I insisted on driving her all the way to Shrewsbury. I appreciated that she might need to gather herself, and not want me under her feet on arriving home; and I said I would only stop for one night. I even offered to leave as soon as I dropped her off, but she wouldn't hear of that, thank goodness, and said that I must stay for that night.

While the meal was cooking, we talked of the near future and I went to look at my diary to remind myself, reluctantly, how soon it would be before we became unavailable to each other. I asked, "When is it you're going away with Hayley?"

"Next Saturday - September first," she said. "And when is it *you're* off to see Felicity?"

"I'm not. Didn't I tell you - change of plans? They're coming to stay with me instead, on Thursday." There was nothing to be added, so I went on to raise something else that had crossed my mind: "You might not want to think about it now, but what would you say to a proper holiday - abroad somewhere perhaps - next year or maybe later this year?"

"You're right - I'm not in the mood to think about something like that just now."

"I said I'd make things up to you, didn't I, for your knee trouble?"

As the meal was coming to a close I raised the subject of the holiday again. I was really just looking for a link, a lead into things I wanted to say.

"Ask me another time," she replied. "In a few weeks preferably!"

"Well," I commented, after waiting in case she wanted to add anything, "at least you haven't said no to the very idea. *A few weeks* - that sounds hopeful, for our future."

"Our future," she echoed - with frustrating ambiguity.

This had to be the moment. "Linda, sweetheart, I've been trying to talk about what happened this morning and its effect on me. I didn't want to make a fuss. . . and get carried away with words. I was so worried that something had happened to you. And, when I saw blood on that stone. . . I think I went mad for a moment. When Tanya came in sight, I thought she was you. I *saw* you. . . the way you used to look, back when we were young. You understand? I hallucinated!"

She reached across the table, looked at me beautiful tenderness, took both my hands and then said something - which I don't remember.

I continued, "I suddenly realised how much you mean to me. The prospect of life without you hit me." I managed to amuse both of us by my next statement: "I'm scared of using the L word, in case you call it a protestation!"

She stood up and said, "Come on - let's go and sit outside - it's a beautiful evening."

We sat, cuddled up, on the two-seater garden bench and watched for the stars to appear. We exchanged corny comments about the time of year and the days getting shorter.

"How long have we known each other," she asked, "this time around?"

"Eight months - I contacted you at Christmas. And I noticed in my diary that it's almost exactly a year since I first contacted Dennis. As you know, that was the start of things - how I came to be aware of you again." While I was speaking a delightful, incense-like scent drifted our way from a distant woody fire.

"Mm. . . I can smell autumn," said Linda. "Bonfires."

A little later I said, "I've just remembered a particular bonfire - or bonfire night. It was in the 1980s when the girls were still with us. Shortly before it, I had been chucking out some stuff of mine from before I knew Maggie, and I came across a firework that I'd kept, unused and over-looked since the 1950s. It was a rocket and it had the price on it - one shilling! From thirty years before, it seemed like something left over from another age. We launched it with great ceremony." I stopped there to think further about that event.

She took her arm from behind me while she twisted round to look me in the face and say, "I can almost read what you're thinking."

"Can you?"

"All that fiery, unleashed potential, sleeping for all those years; and then released. You were thinking it was like us when we met, weren't you?"

"I guess I was."

"Well then, what are we to learn? A rocket streaks off into the sky - brilliant - but only for seconds - meteoric, isn't it?"

"Are you saying that we've had our unexploded fireworks - they're all gone?"

"I don't know. What do you think?"

"I think I can hear Eric warning us not to get enthralled by metaphors."

We both laughed and then lapsed into silence. Then she said, beguilingly, "It *was* fireworks for those first few weeks, wasn't it. Did we use them all up?"

Facing each other, the way we were then, we were placed just right for the long, deep, fierce kiss that followed.

Back inside the house, our talk flowed effortlessly as we gave voice to the things that had previously been understated or unsaid.

At one point, Linda said, "We needed to grow to love each other again."

I thought about that. There was so much truth in that simple statement. Then, having gone beyond any rationality I mused, "If our old love had really gone, I wonder what made us still feel the need for each other."

She looked at me in her amused, forbearing way as she said, "You're trying too hard. We can't make sense of everything."

"Well, I did wonder. Apart from all that leftover limerence, what has kept us hoping in spite of those times we just weren't sure about our feelings."

"Who knows," she said. "As far as I'm concerned it can stay a mystery. And that's enough talk for tonight."

48

I felt surprisingly fresh after the journey home. The views along the A49 had seemed more varied and pleasing than at any time before; and the familiarity of the route had made it untaxing. While I drove I'd been reviewing the year that had elapsed since I was prompted by vague, scented reminiscences to write to Dennis. When I contemplated my life before that, it felt unfamiliar and remote.

I was still feeling the pain of parting. The end of our holiday had been too sudden and abrupt, I complained to myself. If only I could have stayed with Linda for one more day. Much as I looked forward to seeing Felicity and Jim and the boys I had wanted to turn round and go back to her. It reminded me of the separation we had suffered in our distant past, but this time the angst-ridden adolescent emotions had dwindled.

It was still light when I took a walk across the bridge. On the way I stopped to look over the parapet. There were the seasonal streaks and patches of algal foam but they were still - no flow, no movement up or down stream, the tide being near to turning. I thought back once more to that day a year before when I had stopped to look, had been distracted, and had stepped into the flow of cause and effect that had transformed my life.

I remembered it being the fractal patterns that had caught my attention on that occasion. I was very much into fractals at that time, looking for them in clouds and plants and elsewhere in nature. A bit nerdy, I now thought - I'm still interested, but not so concerned any more. From where I stood I could just see across to the wall at the back of my garden, beneath which lay my patch of salt marsh. A new type of plant had appeared on it. Possibly cord grass, I decided - that could be next in the succession - but I was in no hurry to go and check.

Linda phoned at 10.30. I had just gone to bed and so had she, but we were both very much in the mood to talk. We started with the usual ordinary things. She asked about my journey and I asked if she had heard from Sarah, one of whose children had been ill.

She told me all was now well. We then went on to exchange various bits of news that had arrived by email while we'd been away.

"There was a long one from Eric," she said. "You wouldn't believe how much progress he's made."

"So, what progress has he made?"

"Well, he says that the second volume is nearly ready to be published, although he's not sure when that will be. And he's finished the one we were working on when you were there. It's now with Helena for editing."

"What - actually finished? It's only a fortnight or so since you and he were in the thick of it. I hope he appreciates all the help you gave him."

"He does. He said a lot about how grateful he was. I'm just glad he can now devote himself to the last - his living memory part."

"How long will that take to finish?"

"I've no idea. I just hope he lives long enough."

Things went quiet for a moment, following her allusion to mortality. Then I asked, "Will *you* be doing any writing before you go on holiday?"

She almost snorted. "I don't think so! There are too many things I need to think about and do before I go away."

"Holidays," I said, "more trouble than they're worth."

"Well - it may surprise you - I've been thinking about your suggestion of us taking a proper holiday." Pause.

"Any ideas?"

"Yes. Are you really keen on going to foreign parts? Only, I'd like a holiday in London - haven't been there since John died. Suddenly felt like seeing the museums and art galleries, going to the theatre and. . ."

"Brilliant! Just what I'd like to do. We'll need to plan it as soon as possible to make sure we can book places. I'm so glad you suggested that - it's the kind of thing I've been wanting to do but I had no-one to do it with."

"We'll leave Offa's Dyke till next year, shall we - in the spring?"

"Yes. . . How is your knee?"

"Don't know - haven't tested it since we got back."

"I hope we're both still fit enough by the spring."

"We'll have to see, won't we? We can do the walk in little bits."

"What about the present?" I said. "How soon before we can be together again?"

"I've been thinking about that. How about the end of September? I'd like to come to you. We can visit Sarah in Exeter. She's been saying she wants to meet you."

"Sounds good to me. Anyway, back to the future - perhaps we won't always live so far apart." She said nothing in reply and I found that a good moment to broach something I'd wanted to talk about before but hadn't known how to begin. I said, "Do you remember, at Dennis and Gwen's, we were sitting outside, at night, saying how fortunate we were to be in good health?"

"Yes?"

"Well, he went on to comment that you and I might be suffering from - 'decrepitudes' was his word - that he didn't know about. . ."

"Are you worried I'm going to drop dead or suddenly become an invalid?"

"No, no! I wasn't thinking of you. I was thinking of something I ought to own up to..."

"Go on then - confess."

"I had a sort of mini-stroke five years ago. It hasn't happened again; and I've been watching my blood pressure and cholesterol ever since. I thought I ought to mention it."

"If you're not worried about it, I'm not. As far as *my* medical history is concerned, there's nothing yet to report. I've had a couple of scares but there's nothing to fret about at the moment."

"I'm very glad to hear that. I just hadn't thought of you being ill - you seem so... youthful."

This time she did snort. "You're deluded! I've got the little things like aches and pains - what we used to call rheumatism..."

"So have I!"

"Well then. Old age will inevitably creep up on us with all its frustrations and indignities - and more scares, probably, before we peg out. So, *Carpe diem* and all that! And now it's time for this old lady to say goodnight."

"Oh... OK. Goodnight... sweetheart."

"Goodnight and... *sweet* dreams."

We actually went on to say a few more things before sleeping but they were just 'sweet nothings'.

§

Pellitory Books

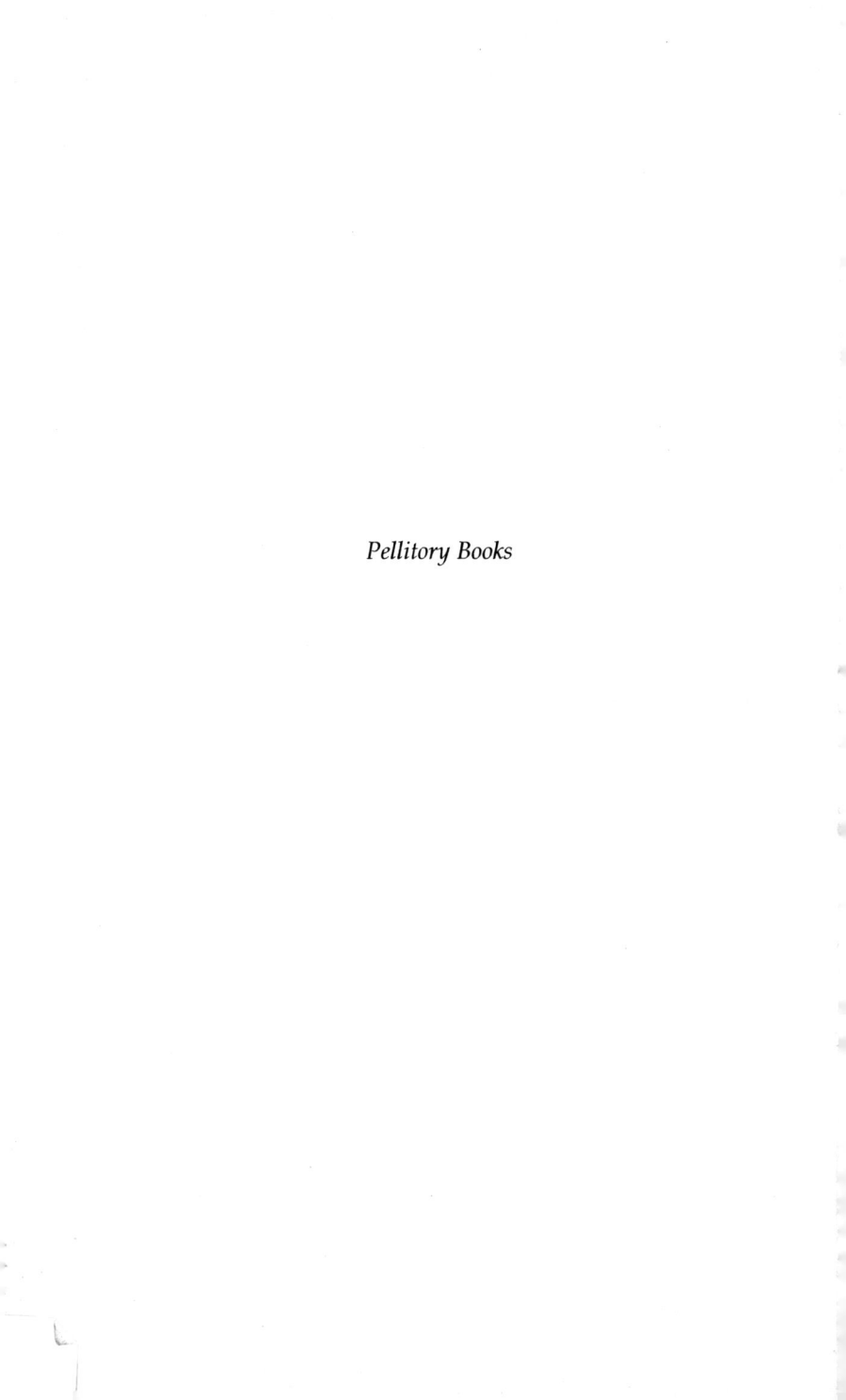